THE FLAT WOMAN

THE FLAT WOMAN

A NOVEL BY

VANESSA SAUNDERS

FC2
TUSCALOOSA

FC2 is an imprint of the University of Alabama Press

Inquiries about reproducing material from this work should be addressed
to the University of Alabama Press

Book Design: Publications Unit, Department of English, Illinois State
    University; Director: Steve Halle, Production Intern: Georgeanne
    Drajin
Cover image: squintpictures/stock.adobe.com
Cover design: Matthew Revert
Typeface: Baskerville URW

Thank you to the following journals for publishing excerpts of this book:
Seneca Review, *Los Angeles Review*, *Western Humanities Review*, *Nat. Brut*,
Entropy, *Passages North*, *A Velvet Giant*, *Poor Claudia*, *The Stockholm Review
of Literature*, *Cleaver*, and *Requited Journal*.

Library of Congress Cataloging-in-Publication Data is available from
the Library of Congress.
ISBN: 978-1-57366-208-6
E-ISBN: 978-1-57366-911-5

For my husband

To be innocent is to be full of contradictions.

—Kim Yideum, *Cheer Up Femme Fatale*,
translated by Ji Yoon Lee, Don Mee Choi,
and Johannes Göransson

On the morning of her ninth birthday, the girl woke up with a rash of bird feathers.

A plate of gray-and-white seagull feathers, thick as a coat of armor, covered her back, from her neck to the base of her spine. It was painful to sit up, painful to lie down, painful to stand on her legs, the feather shafts poking out of her skin.

I'm sorry, Momma said as she left for work, your aunt will be here soon to watch you. By ten a.m., the girl developed a fever so high sweat soaked through her downy coat. Dripping, she tried to walk to the bathroom and saw floating green crescent moons rise from the hallway floor.

Her aunt found her in bed, wet and hot and feathered. Come on, her aunt said, you'll feel better if we go to the zoo.

Feathers mashed in a ball under her sweater, the girl walked with her aunt, hand in hand, staring at the gulls circling the air. Her aunt bought her a hot dog with relish, then they stared at some sea lions lying on a rock. From their glass cage, the sea lions barked and wagged their tails. The girl tried to eat, but her warm tongue just pushed the food around her mouth, unhungry.

Suddenly a flock of gulls descended on them, a blaze of white feathers, dark claws, and throaty squawks. When the gulls tore the hot dog from the girl's hand, her aunt let go of the girl, shrieked. Falling to the ground, her aunt pushed the girl out in front of her. The girl tripped on her shoelace and fell face-first.

The sound of the gulls' wings flapping filled her ears as they followed her down, cutting her knuckle flesh, drawing blood. The girl believed she was going to die, based on the red liquid seeping into the pavement, her aunt's screaming, and the talons scraping the back of her neck. Eventually the sound stopped.

They raised their heads, tentatively. A clear sky.

Her aunt slowly stood up, bleeding from her hands. Her aunt tried to wipe a blood trickle off her arm, but only smeared the rust-colored fluid down her bangled wrist. She gathered her purse. They were trying to get their revenge, she said, for what we've allowed to happen.

They both ran to the car, not wishing to see any more creatures.

PART I

THE GIRL AND HER MOMMA SIT IN FRONT OF THE TELEVISION, WHICH PLAYS THE MORNING NEWS.

Are you sure you don't want to try it? Momma asks.

I don't.

Even movie stars need it you know, her momma says, twisting a strand of hair behind the girl's head, yanking the girl's neck just a little.

The bad guys or the good guys?

Both.

If I had a dad, I wouldn't need it.

Momma doesn't say anything.

If I had a dad, I could sit on his lap and spill out all my feelings. Then I would cry like a baby. If I had a dad, I wouldn't have any issues.

Stop moving, Momma says, *I'm almost done.* The elastic snaps against the girl's hair as Momma secures the hair tie around one braid.

Therapy would toughen your boundaries, Momma says quietly.

The girl doesn't reply. Her attention is already out the window, watching the sea slip in a blue line. The seagulls shrieking in the air above their neighbor's duplex don't seem bothered.

She watches the sun careen across their white feathers. Remembering the scrape of their beaks at the zoo, she curls her fingers into her palms. She looks down at her small, white hands, but nothing changes.

Can I have some hot chocolate?

Turning, Momma steps out of the living room. In the kitchen, the girl hears the fridge creak, milk hitting the saucepan, the click of the stove. After a few minutes, Momma returns to the couch with a mug of steaming hot chocolate, the whipped cream spritzed into a twirl. *Voila*, Momma says and hands the girl the mug. The girl grabs the cup, not moving her eyes from the morning news.

A terrorist attack occurred this morning in the city of Pinecoast . . .

Onstage, the politician delivers a speech. Behind a podium, in a navy suit, he waves his hands in the air. A large crowd surrounds the stage, silent. As he fumbles his words, he dabs the perspiration from his protruding forehead with a handkerchief. The politician crumples the handkerchief and shoves it into his pocket.

Then a falling white streak drops into view. A seagull descending from the sky. The crowd gasps as the bird drops onto the politician's head. In a flash of charcoal-and-white feathers, the gull bounces off his forehead and rolls down his shoulder. The bird spills down his right arm, leaving a trail of cream feathers on the politician's blue suit, before landing on the stage.

The politician stops talking and dusts the bird feathers from his lapel. On the stage, the seagull lies at his feet. Wings splayed, its neck contorted. The camera zooms closer on the gull's eyes, glassy and black. The bird doesn't beat its wings.

Frowning, the politician looks at the bird at his feet, one pink claw suspended upward. When he looks up, he leans closer to the microphone:

We won't let the terrorists get away with this.

The politician smiles and thrusts his fist into the air. The crowd roars as the politician punts the dead bird into the audience. Someone catches the bird with one hand and the surrounding crowd ripples. Smiling, the politician straightens his tie as the crowd erupts.

The girl exclaims, *Ow. You're pulling too tight.*

Momma drops the girl's braids and turns off the TV. *Sorry. You're done. Go grab your book bag.*

Momma is rinsing her face in the bathroom. Momma is gathering her purse on her strong shoulders that are pretty like angel wings. Both of their breaths generate white puffs in the morning air as Momma walks the girl to the bus stop: *Don't forget what I taught you. If you start to feel anxious, inhale through your nose and count to four. Close your eyes if you need to.*

The girl nods.

Momma waits until the bus creates a sighing noise, the creaking of its halted wheels. Riding the bus to the school of water-stained walls and a library that smells of must. The girl enters her classroom, where the boys and girls rustle with papers on their desks, scuffing their plastic sneakers against the floor, clearing their sniffling throats as Mr. Teacher takes his position behind the podium. The class begins their morning chant.

> *I believe the government*
> *Is sparkling and true*

Then Mr. Teacher lifts his palm up and the chanting stops. A hung silence. He says, *Would you like to contribute to class today?* looking down at the girl whose lips remain locked, frozen. She begins to count in her head—one, two, three—while inhaling through her nose. Breathing, she focuses on the red petunias on the windowsill, petals flickering red in the breeze.

Sorry, I was just taking a break, the girl says to Mr. Teacher. Mr. Teacher nods and motions for the class to begin; she breathes and then joins them. Burying her mind in the red petals of the petunias on the sill. Next to the flowers lies the classroom snake. The girl stares at its glistening scales of green, white, and black as the python sleeps beneath a heated lamp. Hearing the snake hiss-breathe inside four walls of glass.

All day the girl hears the python hiss into her eardrums as the red petals of the petunias whisper in her ears. Ignoring the sounds. Ignoring Mr. Teacher standing over her desk all day, squinting down at her work while she tries to solve basic sums.

The day collapses into a sum of images: black pavement, white paper, yellow bus. Before bed, Momma brushes the girl's wet tangles out with a red comb. Before falling asleep, the girl wonders if Momma is right. If she should agree to therapy so she could strengthen her leaky boundaries.

THE FOLLOWING EVENING, HIDING UNDERNEATH HER KITCHEN TABLE, THE GIRL WATCHES TWO BLUE-UNIFORMS SHOUT AT HER MOMMA.

Cowering beneath the table, the girl stares at the blue-uniforms from the waist down. Their tall leather boots tap-tap-tap the tile.

One of the blue-uniforms' fingers drums a coiled copper wire, dangling from his belt. A patch of brown hair covers each of his wide, saggy knuckles.

His trapezoid-shaped badge, speckled in flecks of purplish blood, hangs near his waist. The girl can see the shiny patches of fresh blood on his thigh, can hear Momma's bare feet, her toes striking the tile in syncopated beats. Momma's high-pitched pleas whirr like a siren. In response, the blue-uniforms' voices are thick and rough.

Get on your knees, one blue-uniform orders, *you're being detained on charges of seagull terrorism.*

While Momma kneels onto the tile, she says, *But I'm not a terrorist.* Tears puddle down Momma's cheeks. Momma's pink lips, twisted like wrought iron. The girl edges backward, farther under the table. The blue-uniform sinks down, untwists a long copper wire from his belt, and wraps Momma's feet together.

The girl freezes. She can sense the breeze, which feels oddly cool, as it fondles the potted plant on the table above her. Inhaling through her nose, she counts to four.

Then she kind of sees inside the blue-uniforms, their black damaged skeletons. Faceless, they make sounds with their mouths. The blue-uniform continues to wind the copper wire until Momma's feet are totally secure, so she's unable to run or kick. When he finishes, he nudges Momma to her feet. Hoisting her by the arms, they drag her across the kitchen, her bound legs trailing against the tile.

As the blue-uniforms pull Momma down the hall, she glances back at the girl.

The girl stares back, gripping her teeth against her teeth.

Thawp of the front door—

the girl sprints to the window, where she watches them shove Momma into a white van—

the van zips off.

The girl waits by the window for a few minutes, examining the empty street, waiting for the van to reverse and deposit

Momma on the doorstep. When ten minutes pass and no one comes, her throat starts to feel narrow and thin like a plastic straw. Her breath struggles in her lungs. The girl crawls back underneath the kitchen table, where it is very hard to breathe.

HOURS LATER, HER AUNT ROCKETS INTO THE KITCHEN.

Knock knock, her aunt says as she bursts through the front door. The girl crawls out from beneath the table.

You're here, her aunt says. She retrieves a pack of cigarettes from her purse and shakes it, hearing one loose cigarette rattling inside.

Her aunt bends to light her long, white cigarette on the stove. A zigzag of smoke. The girl follows her outside to the patio beneath a night sky pushed with stars.

When will Momma come back? the girl says. Her aunt sighs, *I don't know. The Brothers of COLA have detained her.* Her aunt spikes a lifeless seagull off the patio with the point of her heel. White feathers fly off its dead body as it streaks across the patio. Poofs of ash lift off its body as it tumbles: gray tufts in the yellow light.

Anyways, her aunt says, *I can't sleep here with you every night, but I'll drop off groceries twice a week and ride the bus with you to school in the morning, just until this whole mess gets figured out.*

Can I come live with you?

Honey, you know there's no room at my place. Plus, you don't want to live in my smelly apartment, do you?

No.

Oh my god, it's happening again.

The girl glances down at her arms. From her wrists to her elbows, her arms are coated in bird feathers. About three feathers thick, ash-stained and slick, they jut out from her skin at odd angles. Her aunt stares at her arms, her red lips coiled into a sneer.

You're . . . leaking, her aunt says.

The girl looks down at the white feathers on her forearms, smeared with gray-and-black ash. Against her skin, the gull feathers feel slimy and cold. Their thick, downy coat makes her wrists heavy, as if her limbs wore a heavy jacket. As she hides her forearms behind her back, the feathery plume starts to throb. Staring at the dead seagull in the yard grass turns her stomach sideways. Her tummy asks to unload itself on the lawn, but instead she bites the inside of her cheek.

The girl begins to count the blades of grass at her feet. One, two, three . . .

Don't worry, it won't last very long, the girl says, voice cracking, face red. Feeling the night breeze tickle the feathers, ever so slightly. She tries to back away from her aunt.

Sorry, I'll try not to stare, her aunt tilts her head down. *Anyway, are you OK? I bet you're scared.*

I just want her to come home.

Don't worry. This will all blow over. No one actually believes your mom's a terrorist. She spreads her lips into a smile then extends one cherry-red claw and strokes the side of the girl's head. Her fake nail scratches the girl's ear. The girl pulls her head away.

A palm tree sways in the yard. The yard grass tickles her stomach lining. On the corner, the electronic doors of the grocery store whoosh open; in her head, the girl can hear the doors wheezing as they open and shut, open, shut.

TWO WEEKS LATER, THE GIRL WAKES ALONE IN HER BEDROOM.

The girl rises in her pink pajamas, stares out her bedroom window at the ocean slithering in a blue line. The sky, industrial and gray, crackles with black clouds. A sharp breeze pushes a gust of wind against the window, smattering a handful of ash against the windowpane.

Reads her aunt's note on her desk: GROCERIES ON COUNTER.

Gliding down the staircase, her toes snag on a loose strand of carpet. The wall is festooned with her ashen handprints. She enters the den, littered with candy wrappers, grocery receipts, and unwashed dishes. On the television, the morning news plays. The tap drips, water rushes through the pipes, and the air-conditioning whirrs.

On the TV screen, an image of the COLA prison appears: tall stone walls guard a series of gray buildings. Three thick, black lines of ash pour out the chimneys as an advertisement jingle plays.

Then the screen switches. A brown-haired news anchor with very plump lips appears behind a desk: *A lake has caught fire near Pinecoast's COLA prison, another event of environmental collapse. In another piece of local news, a classics professor at Pinecoast University is undergoing questioning on suspicions of gull terrorism . . .*

The reporter's voice cuts into the girl's ears like steel whorls. Stepping outside, she can taste the sea, its blue relief, and hear the rattling of animals in the bushes.

Then a bluebird thuds against the seagrass. The sound at first frightens the girl: a sudden falling from the sky and the splatter of its torso against the foliage. The girl apprehends its eyes, glassy with death, its pink tongue peering out of its open beak. A rotting fragrance emanates from its lifeless corpse: a gray smell which expands in her nostrils.

Exhaling, the girl picks up the bird, placing it in a plastic bag, which she knots three times and deposits in the trash can in front of the house. Hoping the plastic will prevent her from internalizing any dead feathers. The dead feathers were the worst. She'd have plastic over feathers any day.

She streams into the kitchen, where sunlight bounces against filthy dishes. Unpacking the groceries, she wets a red apple in the tap, its skin glistening. The girl parts her lips, latching her teeth into its good flesh. Juice squirts across her tongue.

One day, the girl thinks, Momma will come home and cut my apples with her sharp knives. She will stir my hot chocolate and teach me how to ride a bike.

The girl watches an ant crawling across the granite countertop near the stack of dishes. Between its arms, the ant hoists a blade of ash above its head like a diamond ring.

The girl's index finger starts to sing with pain, then the muscles in her finger begin to twitch. First, the patch of skin surrounding the curve of her nail turns a gray color.

Next, the swatch of skin surrounding her knuckles feels papery and thin. Slowly, the skin on her whole finger turns ash gray as the surface of her flesh goes thin and fragile.

Her index finger now the color of the ash blade in the ant's grasp. Her skin the fragile consistency of its ash-trembling surface. She stares at her gray, delicate finger for one long moment before she smashes her hand into the countertop. Her boundaries flicker.

ONE WEEK LATER, THE GIRL WATCHES HER AUNT SING INTO THE END OF A BROOM.

Come on now,
Come on now, starchild . . .

Clutching the broomstick like a microphone, her aunt warbles into one end, her black kitten heels lying a strappy pile near the front door. Red-cheeked, her aunt begins to swing and twirl around the kitchen table, still belting into the end of the broom.

You're the star in my constellation
You're the freckle on my pasty skin

Her aunt's red, frizzled hair flops while her body jiggles. She holds out the broomstick, clutching its straw base and wagging its pointed end in the girl's face.

Join me, she says.

The girl crosses her arms: *I don't want to sing.*

We're not singing, we're cleaning. Inching forward, her aunt jiggles the broom closer to the girl's face. Her eyes, dark and excited, leer out of her face.

The girl backs away, keeping her arms crossed, and gazes out the window. On the lawn lies a white, dead swan, its body twisted in a heap. Flies swarm around the swan's eye sockets.

The girl imagines her mother out there, in the midnight air, carrying a backpack with slits in it. The girl sees the invisible poison releasing itself into the atmosphere. In her mind, she watches the swan inhale the unseeable fumes before collapsing limply into the grass.

Oh, come on, her aunt ejects into the silence. She's no longer offering the girl her fake microphone but holding the broom tall. A lock of red hair has fallen out of her bun and dangles near her face like an apology. The girl keeps her arms crossed.

Her aunt drops the broom to the tile where it falls with a clatter. From the closet, her aunt removes a black, dusty vacuum cleaner. *Let's make this place sparkle*, she says, pressing the vacuum on with her bare foot. When her aunt powers on the machine, its purr overpowers the music, temporarily.

You keep this place filthy, her aunt cries, running the vacuum over the tile. The girl walks to the radio and turns off the music.

At school they say she's never coming home. They say she murdered a bunch of seagulls to get back at the government.

Her aunt's smile flops into a straight line, and she pulls the vacuum close to her body. *I was trying to have some fun. I can't talk about that right now.*

Why can't I visit her in jail?

You need to be in school. You know that.

What are the men in suits saying?

Her lawyers say . . . she's not really a terrorist. That they made it all up because they needed someone to blame.

The girl pictures the faces of the blue-uniforms in the transom window: the coils of copper wire, glinting in the faded sun.

She freezes the scene. Her aunt's long fingers and the smell of her perfume. No wind knocks up her throat.

You don't . . . remember anything important from that day, do you?

Her aunt stops rocking the broom and stands perfectly still.

I don't . . . think so. The girl stabs her nails into her palms.

Hey, her aunt says, putting her arm on her shoulder lightly, *it's alright. It's not against the law to open the front door after someone rings the bell.*

The aunt rubs the girl's arm, scraping her fake nails against her sweater. The girl doesn't say anything. After a few long seconds, her aunt removes her hand, then shrugs. *Don't turn off the music again, OK.*

Her aunt's cell phone shakes in her hand as she looks down to read an incoming text. *I've got to go. Sorry. Next time I'll help you clean more.*

The bushes in the yard whisper and rustle in tongues. Outside the bugs feast on the swan's black eyes. Above the girl's head, the ceiling fan clicks.

The plodding of her aunt's heels against the tile. The drag of her car keys against the wood table, tinkling as they're tossed inside her purse. The velvet coos of her aunt's voice, always softest when she's leaving.

The creak of the front door closing, when her aunt departs, the house drifts into a silence whose magnitude is crude.

THE GIRL SITS IN THE COURTROOM NEXT TO HER AUNT. ON THE COURT FLOOR, HER MOMMA SITS, WRISTS TIED WITH COPPER WIRE.

The judge says, *Today, we address the guilt of the defendant. In advance, I ask any opponents of the court, who wish to deny the validity of the court's opinion, stay silent throughout this hearing. Mr. Prosecutor, are you ready to begin your argument?*

Mr. Prosecutor says, *We are, your honor, thank you. The defendant who sits before us has been charged with conspiracy to commit gull murder. This serious charge alleges the defendant led a cell of gull terrorists: a group of deranged, disturbed women, bloodthirsty and sadistic. This cell is suspected to have murdered over two thousand gulls over the period of thirteen months.*

We have hard evidence linking her to the death of eighty-seven seagulls on the morning of March 27. The gulls were found lifeless in and around LaFritter Park, located just outside our fine city of Pinecoast.

The death of one gull was captured on camera after it fell on the head of Mr. Wattersam during his speech. Eyewitnesses claimed they saw the remaining eighty-six gulls fall from the sky within the same five-minute period.

After careful autopsy, the cause of these gulls' deaths was revealed to be cardiac arrest, due to a foreign chemical agent, which the birds presumably inhaled through the air. At the defendant's domicile, we found a backpack with malicious holes, which the State believes was an instrument of gull murder.

The slits in the backpack were unnaturally carved. The State found residue of poisonous substances around the slits; we have determined these slits were incised to emit noxious fumes into the atmosphere, causing seagull hearts to burst and their bodies to descend dead from the sky.

The accused claims to have been home between seven a.m. and eight a.m. on the morning of March 27. But no witness can attest to her presence there, aside from her daughter.

Just look at the suspect now. Absorb her blank, passionless face. Let the coolness of her features fall over you. This is an unwell woman who prayed for the suffering of birds. This was her ultimate desire: deceit, murder, sadism. This woman, she should suffer. She should suffer like the seagulls were made to suffer: neck snapped into parts, wings shattered, bodies dismembered from the fall, and I–

The judge interrupts, *Thank you, counselor.* He pauses and rubs his chin, then shuffles through papers on his desk. He sweeps a document to the floor; the court reporter sprints to pick it up.

After a brief pause, he says, *Because of the gravity of these charges, I hereby sentence the defendant to the maximum term of twenty years.*

Heckles and boos rave in the crowd. *Women are not scapegoats*, someone screams. Members of the audience begin to stand and shout, except for the girl, who just sits there. Her momma twists her neck to look back at the girl. In a flash, their gazes meet. Momma's eyes are bright like coins as her lips mouth a phrase. The girl throws her arms up in confusion. Momma keeps mouthing the words, but the girl continues to shrug and shake her head.

A blue-uniform yanks Momma to her feet. She shuffles out the exit.

A little tear threatens to slide out the edge of the girl's eye. A cry yawns in her chest, tries to escape as runny tears. Then the grass of the courthouse lawn fills her mouth. She can feel the sharp sprigs poking her cheeks, can taste the dank, dry dirt of the lawn in her throat. She tries to swallow.

Are you alright? her aunt asks.

The girl nods, stifling the grass tickling her throat. She doesn't want to puke grass all over the court floor.

Outside, the courthouse lawn is yellow green. On the lawn, a fight breaks out between a protestor and a blue-uniform. A throng stops to watch. No one seems to look at the girl or her aunt as they pass by, heads down, making their way toward the congested parking lot. They get into the car. They pull out of the parking lot crowded with men in suits, reporters holding cameras, and women waving signs.

Out the car window, the girl sees a single protestor standing on the street corner, apart from the hoard. The protestor wears a white linen dress, sneakers, and a backpack. In one hand, the protestor holds a cardboard sign that says: EXCLUSIVELY BLAMING WOMEN IS A CRIME ITSELF.

From her backpack, the protestor retrieves a can of gasoline, which she unlatches and pours over her head. The protestor's lips crumple, tears flying from her eyes, as she douses herself with gasoline. No one pays attention as the clear liquid streams down the protestor's body, making her white dress translucent, revealing the bare apples of her breasts. As the car rounds the corner, the protestor fumbles with a lighter in her hands. The girl tries to cry out; the car wends around the bend; the image of the protestor fades as the parking lot vanishes.

In her aunt's car, diamonds of sunlight on the dashboard. Her aunt reaches to turn on the radio. Streetlights, trees. The trees are tall and brave. The cool thud of the radio says nothing.

The car parks in front of the girl's house, and her aunt promises to return with groceries in a few days. The girl gets out of the car, feeling the wind blow through her veins, whistling as if her body were hollow.

The front windows of the house remind the girl of human eyes. Inside there is the creak of the door hinge, the squeak of the staircase. The girl imagines her momma walking up the stairs with her. Momma telling her to breathe through her nose, to feel the carpet beneath her feet. She sees years of her life pass in advance: birthdays, sick days, and winter formals all spent in isolation. She climbs into bed, where her cries are ripped from her throat, while the eerie quiet of the house ripples and flows.

PART II

TEN YEARS LATER: THE GIRL, NOW A WOMAN, BOARDS THE BUS NEAR PINECOAST UNIVERSITY AND RIDES IT TO THE PRISON. THERE SHE READS THE RED SIGN OF THE PRISON GATE:

POP'S COLA CANNOT SAVE THE DEPRAVED.

Inside the front office, the woman sets down her leather satchel filled with her trigonometry textbook. She presses the desk bell with a soft fingertip; a bell sound lances the room. Then a blue-uniform stumbles out. Deep black ash stains on the elbows of his uniform.

Please sign in, he commands, shoving a clipboard into her hands before standing up from his desk.

I'll be right back. The blue-uniform exits out the door behind him. Shutting the door, hard, he disturbs a layer of ash silt on the floor. The silt lifts in a gray cloud. For a moment, the woman lingers at the desk, watching the dust settle back onto the floor in gray patches.

I'm prepared to wait, the woman says to the closed door. Inhaling a mouthful of ash, she coughs gray specks into her fist, then wipes her hand on her skirt.

Every month these visits upset her. Retreating into one of the plastic chairs, hearing the clock on the wall tick. Feeling the stare of the man sitting behind her, she tries to focus on the TV on the wall behind the desk, which blares the news.

The news cuts to a photograph of an elderly blonde. Curly hair, sagging old-lady lips, big red glasses.

Around noon, the news anchor says, *a ninety-year-old woman was attacked by five gulls who tore her roast-beef sandwich from her hands. Onlookers watched while the gulls drilled her eyes out. She suffered a stress-induced heart attack and was pronounced dead at the scene.*

The news anchor cuts to a live video of a man labeled, "Gene Livrey's Grandson."

The young man in a red hat says, *We believe Granny was an indirect victim of the seagull terrorists. The hatred they unleashed on the natural world has caused animals to seek revenge. Without gull terrorists, Granny would be alive today.*

The news anchor continues: *Meanwhile environmental activists argue it's not the terrorists but the unchecked destruction of the natural world that has caused–*

The woman averts her gaze, settling on the line of glass sculptures of **POP'S COLA** bottles near the reception desk.

From her chair, she watches water leak from the ceiling— plop, plop, plop. One droplet lands on one of the glass POP'S

COLA sculptures. The sculpture has a woman's curvy hips and small waist. A bead of water rolls down the sculpture's glass hips and melds invisibly into the tile. The man in a white T-shirt pops his bubble gum in the chair behind her.

The news continues to blare on the TV, the words faded and jumbled and mute, refusing to enter the woman's head. Minutes slip down the yellowing walls. A heavyset blue-uniform walks past her plastic chair, murmuring into his walkie-talkie; she listens to his black boots squeak against the tile. She remembers watching the blue-uniforms tap-tap-tap their shoes, their black skeletons as they wrapped copper wire around Momma's ankles, the white van barreling away.

The memory makes the air go tight in her lungs. The shoe-shaped water stain in the ceiling blurs. As her heart pulses against her ribs, her what-if questions begin to escalate. What if the last thing she saw on this earth was the face of a blue-uniform while she laid dying on the cold tile? What if they allowed the man popping bubble gum to fornicate with her dead body while onlookers paid to watch?

Helloooo, helloo?

A blue-uniform is standing above her. In a haze, she can only make out his brown, thick mustache.

Knock, knock, young lady, you there? His crotch, right near her face, smells like moldy food.

She stands, slightly dizzy, and follows him as he saunters behind the desk and sits behind the computer.

I wasn't sure if I needed to call a doctor, he jokes as he wiggles the mouse and squints at the computer screen. As he speaks, she notices a line of spittle dangling from his lower lip. When he smiles, the spit quivers but doesn't drop.

What's your mom's name again?

Shirley Jones, she whispers. In the plastic chair, the man in a white T-shirt pops another pink bubble.

Say it louder please.

Shirley Jones, she raises her voice, worried the man behind her has heard her mother's name. A little error like this might result in him following her home or finding her address on the internet. She only recently stopped receiving letters from men requesting her mother's hand in marriage. Apparently, something about a captive, so-called psychotic woman made lonely men very hot.

A hah. The blue-uniform types the name into the keyboard. He peers at the screen for a few moments, then announces, *Well, I can't find that name on our list.* He licks his lips, siphoning the spit back into his mouth.

I visit her every month, the woman offers.

Young lady, he glances at her above his spectacles, *if she's not on the list, she's not here.*

The blue-uniform licks his bottom lip. She rearranges her mouth to speak. He smiles. She swallows, afraid to fuss or call out. So instead of complaining, she spins around and heads for the door. She can feel the eyes of the bubble gum man follow her to the exit.

Scuttling out the waiting room, she hears the bubble gum man's voice in her head: *Shirley Jones. So, you're the daughter of the most sadistic seagull terrorist in the history of Pinecoast. Wowza, I'm impressed.*

My mother's innocent, she snarls out loud. The blue-uniform behind the desk looks at her quizzically just before she slips out the door.

Outside the prison, the woman spots Momma standing in one corner of the yard. *Momma*, the woman yells from the walkway. Momma raises her arm and starts to walk toward the fence.

Her momma ambles toward the chain-link fence slowly, shoulders hunched. Her hair, gray and greasy, lays flat on her scalp. Her cotton candy–pink jumpsuit reads POP'S COLA across the breast.

Up close, the woman can see ash smears around Momma's neck and mouth. Momma grabs a diamond of fence with her ash-soaked fingers. Looking her daughter in the eye.

I'm smaller, Momma says hoarsely, her jumpsuit billowing around her body.

What?

I said I've been mixing chemicals, Momma says, her pink tongue darting behind her stained lips.

I'm sorry. I have something to ask you.

Her momma scrutinizes the security guards at the opposite corner of the prison yard. *I don't have time to chat. I have to go clean sugar beets.*

Can it wait?

We have to make a new batch of COLA syrup by morning.

An alarm blows through the yard, the sound of pennies shaken inside a glass jar. The sound smacks against the side of Momma's face.

See, Momma coughs, *I can't stay.*

I'll come by next week.

Sure, Momma says, turning away. Momma's pink slippers scrape against the concrete as she shambles toward a gray building in the distance. There Momma joins a long line of female prisoners in baby pink jumpsuits. After a few minutes, the alarm rings again. The line of pink women begins to shuffle inside the gray building. Within minutes, ringlets of black smoke flow out of the chimney.

Exiting down the walkway, the woman is distracted. Passing

through the administration buildings of the blue-uniforms, she puts one foot in front of the other. She doesn't smell the mold behind the walls or taste the ash and fumes she breathes through her nose.

She stalks into the parking lot. Near the shuttle stop, two seagulls lay sprawled face down. Stripped of their feathers, their pale skin a pink blot on the asphalt. She waves her hand in front of her face to shake the smell of their flesh cooking in the sun. Bird toast, she jokes to herself, picturing the man with the bubble gum slapping his knees with laughter.

Suddenly, she freezes and waits. What if her skin becomes bird toast? What if she sees her trigonometry professor on the shuttle when her skin is pink, featherless gull flesh? What if the smell lingers? What if she never loses her virginity because she reeks of cooked bird?

Standing there in the strong sunlight, she tries to shut her feelings off. It's like turning down the dial of a radio. Sunshine. Sea air. A random lawn. She breathes through her nose, looking up at the cement prison exterior.

The sunlight casts long prison shadows across the parking lot.

TWO WEEKS LATER, STEPPING OUT OF HER COLLEGE DORM, THE WOMAN BRUSHES SHOULDERS WITH A TALL GUY WHO DOESN'T GLANCE BACK.

Descending the brick steps, the woman steps on something wet. Something crunches, something slides. Expecting a patch of soggy leaves, she sees a dead crow on the bottom step.

Wet, red blood. Its torso has been cut open with a knife: lungs, bones, exposed cartilage. Its cut chest reveals its vulnerable, red heart; small, white lungs; the yellow coil of its intestines. Her bare feet, exposed in sandals, are covered with bloody marks—like a painting from a famous artist. The crow's shattered ribs lie in shards near her feet.

With her next step, her sandals slide on a scrap of bone. She wobbles but doesn't fall.

She looks up. Across the grass, there they are. A clump of girls, giggling behind their hands. Tricia from trigonometry, Martha from her dorm hall. They glance away, then stare back at her. She almost hears their thoughts in her ears. *Your momma is a psycho,* they're saying. *Your momma is sick, she killed birds. Bet she gets it pretty bad in the cage. We left the bird especially for you.*

She counts the number of surviving bones in the crow's chest. Three on each side. The bones thin like toothpicks or miniature flutes. Maybe it's a coincidence. A prank for anyone to step on. The woman keeps her expression flat, though her cheeks redden. Kicking the crow down the steps, not glancing again at the girls.

She concentrates, trying to keep her boundaries from leaking. Focusing. Focusing on her blood-smeared feet. Not thinking. Not thinking about the dead crow she just kicked down the brick steps. Not thinking about its blood-wet feathers. Its black, dead feet, its little broken beak.

Her shoulders tense—she imagines the black feathers bursting through her arm skin. Covering her forearms with gleaming, wet, black-red feathers. The smell of blood, which always reminded her of rust. She imagines the girls giggling like hideous birds. *Feathering freak*, they'd cry out. Suddenly she sees the whole school on the lawn, laughing as she flaps her feathery arms. She closes her eyes, bites her lip.

Then she hears a screech in the dormitory parking lot.

One hundred feet away, the woman sees her aunt's cherry-red car park in the lot. Exiting, her aunt waves, hair spinning, then slams the car door. Scuttling across the yellow lawn, her aunt grabs her hand: *C'mon, let's go for a drive.*

Alright.

The woman gets in. The car pulls out of the parking lot, tires scudding against pavement, attracting dirty looks from students eating lunch in the quad.

As the car pulls out the lot, the woman's thoughts spin: What if the car smashes into a tree? What if the wheel pops off my aunt's car and I miss class? What if I break my legs and am forced to drag myself back to campus until I'm scabbed and ugly?

To soothe herself, the woman starts to count the redwood trees they pass. She imagines chopping the trees down with her hand. One, two, three . . .

What are you thinking about? her aunt says.

Nothing. Did you do something to your hair?

Yes.

What's going on? I have class soon.

I brought you something. One hand on the wheel, her aunt retrieves a cupcake with baby blue frosting wrapped in wax paper. As her aunt digs the cupcake out of her purse, she curses, seeing the frosting smeared on the sides of her bag. The car swerves, almost barreling into a pedestrian.

The woman shuts her eyes and braces herself by gripping the armrest, but when she opens her eyes, the car is back on the road. Her aunt straightened the wheel at the last possible moment.

Congrats on almost finishing your first year of college. And at the top of your class, her aunt says. *All this with your mom in prison. That's impressive.*

Thank you.

I thought we could celebrate. You wanna go to the zoo?

I have a final today. I can't.

Your loss. Her aunt taps her acrylic nails against the steering wheel, but her voice isn't upset. *Anyhoo.* She twirls a piece of red hair around her finger. *Are you sure you don't want to go to jail? Sorry, I meant back to college. In the fall.*

The woman's posture doesn't change, but the muscles in her neck tighten.

It's OK. And I'm sure. I want to take a year off. I don't like living on campus.

Those girls still giving you trouble?

Today it was a dead crow for me to step on.

Oy.

I want to switch schools. Or wait a year.

But don't you think that'll happen wherever—

I want to switch schools. Or wait a year.

OK . . . the turn signal beeps as the car waits at a light.

Well, her aunt says, *you know it's your choice if you want to take some time off. Or switch. When you do go back to college, you'll do just as good. Brains. Just like your mother . . . she was always better at school than I was. Though if I'd worked harder . . . who knows.*

As they wait at the light, a white **POP'S COLA** van bumbles down the road. Lacquered on the side of the van, there is a pink outline of a curvaceous woman. As the car passes, her aunt stays silent as she tightens her grip against the steering wheel, pressing her nails into the spongy leather. The light turns and her aunt accelerates to the right.

When she speaks, her aunt's voice is high and shrill: *You know, if you take a year off, you'll lose your work-study job. And if you move, you'll forfeit your scholarship. Without that money, you'll be broke. Flat broke. And I don't have the means to help out.*

When the woman looks into her aunt's face, she sees her dark eyes swimming in her head like black holes.

Her aunt clears her throat and lowers her voice. *I'll pay you back for that other stuff* . . . she flaps her hand. *As soon as I can.*

What are you saying?

Sell the house, get a job, or stay in school.

Words swim in the woman's brain while her aunt continues to babble. Scholarship. Brains. House.

Again, I don't mean to be harsh, but your financial situation is . . . really bad . . . your savings will last for a few months, and then . . .

Other palpable memories struggle to rise, while her aunt talks; gashes or flickers the woman breathes through. She licks her lips and tastes dirt. She smiles at her aunt, as if nothing is awry.

There is one other option, her aunt says.

What?

A sugar daddy. You know what that is right?

I know what the term means.

It's pretty great. Don't ask me how I know this. But you should consider it. She reaches out and taps the woman's hands three times with her acrylic red nails. The car swerves again to the right. *You need some . . . generational wealth in your life. You didn't really have parents, after all.* She smiles, showing a cherry-red lipstick line on her teeth.

I guess your issue will be finding someone who likes . . . the outdoors. With your situation and all. Someone . . . understanding . . .

Did you ever figure out if it was your boundaries making you anxious? her aunt continues. *Or does your anxiety make your boundaries leak? I know your mom was a big fan of the talking cure . . .*

The woman stops hearing her, instead watching the furry limbs of the redwood trees, verdant and sharp green, disappear through the car window.

The car screeches to a stop in the parking lot. *Anyhoo, that's my advice. Get a job. I love you. I'm not able to help you move next weekend.*

The woman exits, *I love you too. And that's alright.*

Outside the car, the woman pauses in the parking lot, waving as her aunt's scuffed, red car shoots down the street. As her aunt's car recedes, the woman surveys the empty road leading away from Pinecoast University. She hears the wind rattle the branches over her head as a slow cloud falls over the sun. She surveys the parking lot: vacant, aside from a crumpled seagull-terrorist poster pushed around by the wind.

To soothe herself, she closes her eyes. In the blackness, she conjures a vision of a yellow house she saw in a movie about a happy family. In the yellow house, she wouldn't be poor. She sees herself on the front porch of the house, watching the breeze rustle the purple tulips.

AFTER MOVING OUT OF THE DORM, THE WOMAN WALKS INTO THE GROCERY STORE NEAR HER MOMMA'S HOUSE. SHE ASKS IF SHE MAY SPEAK WITH MR. MANAGER AND HE BECKONS HER INSIDE HIS CRAMPED OFFICE.

The woman sees posters of naked women licking ice cream cones or gripping enormous wads of beef between two seeded slices of bread. In their small hands, the food is blown out of proportion: the ice-cream cone is the size of one female's head, her full pink lips parted as spit spools out from her mouth. These posters coat every available space of his office wall.

So what can I do for you today? he relaxes into his armchair. On his desk lie a stapler, a computer, and a large black notebook.

His nametag says Mr. Manager in red letters. The woman hands him a copy of her résumé, says she has no experience but she's willing to learn, that she's hardworking and taking a short break from school . . .

A cramp in her stomach. Then a bloated feeling in the gut as the pain spreads to her teeth and gums. She stops talking, putting her hand on her stomach. She bends at the hip, trying to suppress the sensation in her tummy.

Is everything alright? His words are hard and quick.

She tries to say yes, but instead a full feeling expands in her throat. Holding her mouth shut. As a final effort to keep herself from puking, she slaps her face. Mr. Manager studies her, eyes flashing, and his desk chair squeaks as he scoots it back three inches. As she places her hands on her knees and succumbs to the pressure trying to release out of her mouth.

Pinpricks poke her throat as she opens her jaw. Ten staples fly out from her lips onto the office floor. In a pile, their metal lines gleam. After the objects have been evacuated from her mouth, she barfs up a fistful of bloody spit.

Mr. Manager leaps from his chair and grabs the stapler from his desk. Brandishing it behind his head, he raises his voice.

Get out. He motions to the door with his stapler.

What? She tries to pretend like she doesn't know what's happening.

I don't know if this is a weirdo prank or some terrorist shit. Get out of my office now before I call the blue-uniforms, freak.

She gulps, sweat collecting on her neck and forehead. As shame pricks the insides of her cheeks, she stalks down the hallway. On her way out, she passes a poster of a woman, headless, naked, legs splayed. What if Mr. Manager follows me to my car and beats me senseless? she thinks. As she hurries down the hallway, the word *freak* reverberates in her head.

In the produce aisle, the cold air makes her hair rise from her arms. She shivers, staring down at her feet, and almost walks into a pile of bananas. When she looks up, she sees a man. Across the aisle, he's slumped against a freezer. Wearing a suede jacket with tassels hanging from his shoulders, he leans against the cold freezer door, shoving a fistful of apple crisps into his mouth.

Adjusting his gaze, he notices the woman, paused near the bananas. The grocery store light beams across his forehead skin; he swallows and shows the woman his pearly whites.

Watching the woman freeze, he tilts his head and meets her gaze.

She feels her footsteps, separate from her thoughts, pull her body in his direction.

She stops, sucks in a breath. As she passes the frosty glass of the fridge door, she scrutinizes her reflection, pushing a strand of hair behind her ear.

To move across the fluorescent aisle

drawn by the curious image of a man reposed

and snacking on a bag of apple crisps.

The woman stops in front of the freezer. Back slumped against the cold glass, the man pops another apple crisp into his mouth and looks at her. His breath smells sweet and ripe like fruit. As he reaches into the bag of crisps, the brown tassels on his jacket sway; underneath it, he wears a cream dress shirt. Three undone buttons expose his tan chest with several curly brown hairs. His chest glistens as if oiled.

Hey Mr. Man, could you please move over?

The man straightens and steps away. As the woman retrieves a bag of frozen mangos, he adds, *You don't have to call me Mr.*

When she tries to speak, no words crest on her lips at first, then she says, *Thank you.*

The woman blinks; with her eyes momentarily closed, the image of his white shirt singes the dark beneath her lids. The man retrieves a piece of paper from his pocket. As he hands it to her, their fingers graze briefly.

Here's a pamphlet I helped write about the bird issue, he says. *This is genuine information.*

Thanks. She studies the picture of a seagull on the cover and the title labeled "Grief Patterns." *This looks interesting,* she says.

We could talk about it sometime.

That would be nice.

I'm playing a show at the Pig tomorrow if you'd like to come. He hands her another piece of paper, waxy and folded in half, which she accepts.

That's your band, she points to the image on the poster. On the poster, the man is pictured with a leather jacket, two guys, and a drum set.

I'll be there, she says.

She looks up. The man grins. His teeth are perfectly straight, white like pearls.

See you at the Pig, he says.

THE WOMAN AMBLES HOME, ENVISIONING THE MAN'S
BRIGHT TEETH, WHICH FLOAT UP IN HER MIND LIKE
A MIRAGE. BEFORE BED, SHE UNFURLS THE MAN'S POSTER
AND TACKS IT TO HER BEDROOM WALL. THEN SHE OPENS
THE PAMPHLET AND BEGINS TO READ.

Increasing rates of environmental change, alongside the sharp increase in atmospheric pollution, have resulted in unprecedented levels of bird death. For this reason, the grief patterns of birds have become a hot topic in bird science.

The situation is grave. In the tropics last month, ten thousand birds were discovered dead. Scientists think the sudden death of these birds was caused by a cloud of ash in the jungle, suffocating them. A group of ornithologists spread a net in the tropics, hoping to entrap some survivors.

Operating under the assumption that the remaining birds had lost someone they loved, they caught the surviving birds in nets. Then, using long, painful needles, scientists injected the grief-filled birds with sedatives. The birds went straight to sleep. They implanted tracking devices in the birds' chests.

When the mourning birds arose from their comas, they flew. The tracking devices allowed the scientists to trace their migratory routes.

Grieving birds stayed in the air; they did not stop. From the Pacific Northwest to the Himalayas to the Artic Circle.

They roam the world only to return to the place where they began. So the grief pattern of a bird is relentless flight. This is the only known grief pattern of a bird.

The woman shreds the pamphlet into pieces, ripping the phrase "grief patterns" in half wherever it appears. Some of the strips she releases onto the floor by her bed. The rest she shoves in her mouth and swallows in one gulp, feeling the hard paper scrape down her throat.

THE WOMAN GOES TO THE MAN'S SHOW. SHE ENDS UP NEAR THE STAGE, SMUSHED NEXT TO A STATUE OF A PIG.

The man squeezes the neck of the microphone. Over the bump bump of the drum, he's singing:

> *Gulls fall extinct*
> *From the sky*
> *Thanks pollution*
> *Altered planet*

In the dark crowd, the woman claps. Her eyes stick to the stage. She stretches her arm out toward him as blackness splits in the space between her fingers.

> *The government will only deflect blame*
> *Point fingers*
> *In the wrong direction*
> *Can't they see*
> *We're all in jeopardy*

Her pulse beats in her ears. The music blares from the speakers. On the stage, the yellow spotlight glows on the man's face.

In this material world
My habits are all wrong
Seagull, you're soft
And so perfect

Behind her, someone touches her back. Their fingers dig into the waistband of her panties and pinch the soft of her butt. She spins around. Five men are pressed close to her; the crowd is a mass of limbs and mouths and sounds. In the dark she squints, cheeks flushed. But no one meets her eyes. There is no clear body attached to the hand. There is no one to say, *Please, don't touch me, sir.*

So she shoves her way through the crowd, jamming her elbows into hips. She finds a group of women to stand between and adjusts her gaze.

Our government
Doesn't care about your body
Doesn't care about the planet

As the song ends, the woman traipses outside for a breath of fresh air. A guy dressed in a rouge-colored suit leans against a concrete wall. Smoke rolls out of his nostrils. The guy says, *Hey, sugar, you got a boyfriend?* She says, *I'm married*, and then her mouth hangs open. A streetlight hanging over her head flickers. In the darkness, she lets a manic grin spread across her face. As the woman retreats into the writhing crowd, she thinks she wouldn't mind having a home again.

FOR THEIR FIRST DATE, THE MAN AND THE WOMAN HEAD TO A CASINO. IN THE LOBBY, THEY GAZE AT A POSTER FOR A FAKE BEACH. THE MAN SAYS, LET'S GO. SHE NODS. THEY SIT DOWN NEAR A WAVE MACHINE.

Thanks for taking me out, she says. *Your music was awesome the other night.* Her dress sleeve swirls glissando as she staunches her chin with her hand, catching the man meeting his own eyes reflected across the wave machine.

I've never been to a fake beach before, the woman offers. A couple saddled in beach loungers clinks two margarita glasses on the artificial shoal. Plastic waves shoot out with a hiss every thirty seconds, stretching across the sand. With each protrusion, the wave machine rattles and hisses and shakes. People in tropical shirts lounge in tropical chairs, watching the plastic waves shoot out of the machine.

I think this place used to be a bowling alley, the man says. The woman squints. She could almost see where the lanes used to be, camouflaged with sand heaps, fake rocks and papier-mâché seaweed.

A lady in a turquoise mermaid's tail and scallop-bikini bra lays on top of one of the fake barnacles. Every two minutes, the mermaid emits a long warbling moan.

The man raises his eyebrows and they both chuckle into their hands. When the waitress appears, the woman orders a virgin piña colada. After their drinks arrive, he begins to jabber about changes in the weather and knocks his alligator boot against his chair. The woman struggles to listen, watching his lips move over the white line of his teeth.

Is everything alright? The man stops talking. The woman presses her fingernails into her palms.

Yes, she says quickly.

You seem distracted.

I'm listening, promise.

Tell me about your interests.

A fear swims in the woman's gut. A fear of speech—to speak too loud, too sure, too bossy. Afraid of the volume of her own presence. Her hands holding her drink start to tremble. When she speaks, she's sure to keep her voice low and even.

I like to read, she says quietly.

To her relief, he nods. *Me too.*

She crosses her legs. Tightening her thigh muscles, her body squeezing against her body. The man allows his finger to brush against her finger. She clears her throat, not used to being touched. But she doesn't move her finger. She allows it to stay there, skin on skin.

Finally she says, *What else do you do for fun?* He says, *Aside from music?* She bobs her head.

I studied philosophy in school, he says. *Graduated four years ago with honors. Now I work as an environmental activist. Run a few different groups, connect people together, organize marches, all that.*

He readjusts his spine against the wave machine; shaking, it spits out a roll of blue plastic. With one hand, he pushes a lock of brown hair out of his eyes. He squints down at her hands as she drums her fingers against the tabletop.

You sure you're OK?

Yeah.

I understand it's a little traumatic for women—all the terrorism stuff. We don't have to talk about it. Do you want to see a song I wrote about you?

The woman brightens, *Yes.*

This is only the beginning. He digs into his leather man-purse. Spreading the crumpled paper across the table, the lyrics read:

> *You are sweet and scrumptious*
> *Girl in the frozen aisle*
> *Caught my eye*

Next to the bananas
Do you wanna
Go steady?

Is this a real question? she asks, looking up. His eyes are round and blue and bright.

The man shakes his head up and down.

Yes, she yelps, almost knocking over her piña colada.

They smooch.

THE WOMAN WAITS IN THE WAITING ROOM OF THE COLA PRISON TO HEAR HER MOTHER'S NAME CALLED. FINALLY, A BLUE-UNIFORM LEADS HER DOWN A SERIES OF SERPENTINE HALLWAYS TOWARD THE VISITING AREA.

You're here, Momma says. Her hands, wrapped in copper wire, lie on top of the table. Her eyes move back and forth across the woman. Momma's pink jumpsuit, stained with gray ash on the chest and arms. The woman starts to lay her hand gently on top of Momma's bound hands. Looking down at Momma's calloused fingers, a half-moon of black grit beneath one fingernail, the woman freezes.

Instead of touching Momma, the woman places her hands under her legs. Hunching forward, the woman shivers.

I wanted to tell you I'm taking a break from school.

You're kidding.

The woman doesn't continue. Instead, she listens to the room, chattering and loud, the steel tables filled with prisoners in pink, their well-dressed daughters sitting across from them. The woman looks at the daughters: their lovely skirts, manicured nails, and neatly braided hair.

The woman looks back at her momma. *I have a boyfriend now*, the woman offers. *A real one*. She clears her throat and stares into Momma's eyes, which are no longer moving. Suddenly Momma's eyes stay very still.

He took me golfing yesterday. This weekend we're going to the movies. I wanted to come here and tell you.

Well, Momma says.

Momma licks her bottom lip and opens her mouth, preparing to speak. A stutter in her throat, she licks her lips again.

Momma shifts her head to the right and focuses on the wall behind the woman. Her eyes, once blue, look faded as white pearls. *I don't think they're ever going to let me out of here*, she says.

But your sentence is up in ten years.

I said I don't think they're going to let me out of here, her mother raises her voice. All the chatting around them stops. Necks crane, heads turn in their direction. Hands trembling, Momma tries to flick a speck of ash from her eye with the edge of her tied hands. It takes her half a minute, but eventually her fingertip finds the black spot near her tear duct.

The woman's hands move to clasp her momma's fingers, which are shaking, the copper wire rattling against the steel table. But as soon as she closes her soft finger around Momma's dirty thumb, the skin red and flaking, a blue-uniform screams out. He walks up quickly and swats the woman's hand with a black belt.

No touching, he says gently as her hand stings. *And your time is up.*

Momma's eyes quiver as the woman rises to follow the blue-uniform. As he starts to usher her back down a series of hallways, the woman turns and waves goodbye. In the dull prison light, Momma's face looks gray. Momma doesn't raise her bound hands, but she does stare at the woman, dazed, lips twitching. Stepping forward, the woman remembers their shared gaze the day the blue-uniforms dragged Momma out of the kitchen.

THE MAN KNOCKS ON THE WOMAN'S DOOR. WHAT'S GOING ON, SHE ASKS IN THE DOORWAY, I THOUGHT WE WERE GOING TO THE BEACH TOMORROW.

Well, my dog, Sartre, died last night, he leans into her. His lips part, a low rumbling. Embracing him, her hand grazes the back of his neck, which is burning hot.

What happened?

Sartre ate too much chocolate cake, he says, leaning into the woman. *He gobbled the cake up while it was cooling on the stove. I forgot dogs are allergic to chocolate.*

I'm sorry for your loss, she says. She turns away, leading the man down the hallway and into the den, where she kicks a soda can under the couch and picks up a pair of her underwear and stuffs it under the cushion.

Sorry, I wasn't expecting anyone.

I don't mind a little mess. It makes it homey.

Wincing, she flicks on the television.

A fly buzzes in the air near the man's head. He swats at it with his hand. The woman asks if he wants some tea, he says yes, so she slips into the kitchen. While she heats the water in a saucepan, she removes some of the dirty dishes from the sink and hides them in the cupboard. After a few minutes, she pours the boiling water into a mug.

When she returns to the living room, he jumps up to make room, knocking the lamp with his elbow.

Jolted by his sudden movement, the lamp falls to the ground. The lamp clatters against the floor, the glass lightbulb spreading out as shards. The eggshell-colored lampshade, loose from its wire halo, gets crushed against the glass door.

The woman stares at the dismembered lamp. She remembers her mother flicking the lamp on before cartoons. Nights when Momma used to comb her wet hair into clean, smooth ribbons.

Shit, the man says. He jumps up, kneels, starts to pick up the broken glass with his bare hands. The woman closes her eyes and sees the glass amputating his finger, his index reduced to a bloodied stub.

Stop, she raises her voice, *Please stop. I'll deal with it later.* She sets the hot mug on the end table.

OK. The man hiccups and returns to the couch.

There, he lays his hand on her belly. Her whole body slows.

In her stomach, she feels a wiggling. As if a million tiny centipedes were buzzing in her abdomen. Without attracting the man's attention, she places her hand on her stomach to confirm what she knows: her boundaries are leaking. Her neighbor's goldfish are currently swimming in her stomach.

One hand on her intestines, she can feel the fish pecking and snacking on her pasta dinner. The nausea hits her brain. Stifling the desire to vomit live fish onto the carpet, she tries not to move. Any motion agitates the goldfish, who become spry when disturbed. Her thoughts start to spiral as she looks down at the man's hand, which is also on her belly.

What is that? he says.

What?

That feeling in your stomach.

I don't feel anything. Maybe it's indigestion? Inhaling short, staccato breaths. She can feel wet, slimy scales slipping up her esophagus—as the fish try to crawl up her throat. She counts to four, holds her breath. She pictures their orange fins flopping on the carpet; the man's face revolted; his body running out the door; his black car fading into a pinprick.

Brows furrowed, he removes his hand from her stomach. He pushes it through his hair, then relaxes his shoulders into the couch. When he doesn't say anything more, her breath evens. Her throat relaxes, her airway clears. She takes a deep, full breath.

Her television shouts, *Do you wanna be Elvis? If yes, come to High Plains, where you can live like the King. It's our world-famous All-Elvis enclave.*

The man's gaze smarts on the fake Elvis on the screen. Fake Elvis's limbs ooze across the stage, the spotlight trilling him, grind and pop, blue-light infinity, bedazzles, his smooth limbs lurch, they swing and glissade, Elvis, he opens his jacket, he swags around the stage, migrating his hips. The spotlight shimmers on Elvis's black hair. Elvis's white jumpsuit unzipped to his belly button, showing off his chest hair.

Suddenly the man's breath is regular.

The act of holding is really an unloosening.

THE WOMAN WAITS FOR HER AUNT AT HILDA'S.

Sipping watery coffee from a stained mug, the woman watches her aunt cross the parking lot. Near the steps, her aunt trips on the belly of a gull, its wings scattered like open scissors and face partially smashed. A teaspoon of ash plumes out of the bird's throat and stains the pointed toe of her aunt's heel. Her aunt removes her shoe and shakes it clean.

That dead bird spat ash all over my heel, her aunt says as soon as she sits down. *You'd think they'd figure out a better way to make soda by now.*

I hope they aren't ruined, the woman says, hearing her voice squeak. At the edge of her eyes, the woman spies the waitress flinging the gull into the dumpster. Trying not to imagine herself puking up black feathers on the coffee shop floor, she turns away from the window. Her aunt rips the heads off three sugar packets. One by one, she pours each of them into her coffee.

You look different, her aunt says, stirring her black coffee in the white mug. *Have you lost weight?*

It's a new dress, the woman says, *it's secondhand. My boyfriend took me thrifting.* Her aunt crumples her lips, *That's nice. What's his deal?*

He's a musician. And an activist.

Congrats. Sounds like a cold glass of water. She sips her coffee. *How's the job search?*

I'm still looking.

Time is ticking. Assuming your little boyfriend isn't paying your bills.

I'll find a job. Don't worry.

The TV mounted on the wall displays an image of a female body in a bra and underwear, oiled, positioned on a dinner plate. An advertisement jingle plays. Her aunt says, *Don't you think it's a little funny you're dating an activist?*

Swallowing, the woman says, *I guess so.*

The waitress approaches them to ask if they would like anything else; her aunt glances at the woman and says no.

What are you doing today? the woman says.

Going to run errands. Then I'll get my nails done with Bertha and we'll go to the bars. Oh, I almost forgot. Her aunt opens her white leather purse.

Here are some flowers I got you.

The aunt hands the woman three yellow roses with stems of varying lengths.

The woman smiles. *Thanks.* Rubbing one soft petal with her thumb, she says, *Why is there dirt on these petals?*

I might have picked them from a neighbor's yard. I know how you like . . . this type of thing.

Bringing the flowers to her nose, the woman inhales the dirt of the garden and its accompanying scents. Wind, perfume, a little rot.

I was hoping I could sleep at the house tonight, her aunt adds. *Things with D. have been sticky. I wouldn't get home until real late. You'd hardly notice I was there.*

Sure, the woman says, *I was going to sleep at his place anyways.*

Relaxed, the woman smells the roses, her head totally buzzing.

THE WOMAN AND THE MAN LIE ON HIS BED, WATCHING TELEVISION. THEN THE WOMAN'S PHONE BEEPS WITH A TEXT MESSAGE.

Wanna grab coffee next week? Lv, Auntie.

At first the woman closes her phone and places it on the night-stand. Then she picks it up and begins to type.

Sure, the woman texts back, *I'd love that.*

The man leaps off his bed. As he begins to lower himself onto the carpet, the woman says, *What are you doing?*

The man says, *I have a question to ask you.* She stands and he sinks to the floor. On the carpet, he's kneeling on one leg, grinning wide. Her heartbeat thickens as an anticipatory smile spreads. She tries to freeze the moment in her mind.

Yes, she tries not to shout.

Wait. You haven't heard what I'm asking.

OK ask. She feels blood barrel through her body, as electricity trickles up her legs and into her chest and face.

Will you move with me to High Plains, Nevada?

A hot pause. He doesn't have anything in his hands. The electricity in her runs cold, a shard of glass. She stares at his yard through the sliding-glass door: the yellow lawn, the desiccated vines, the clouds tumbling low across the sky.

Her vision lands on a lifeless hummingbird near the flower bed. Its piquant, red feathers, attracting her eyes like a bullseye. After a second, she shifts her head down at the man—not wanting her boundaries to act up.

He continues: *I've been offered a position at the All-Elvis enclave.*

Elvis? she says. Her lips struggle for the right expression, shoulders slumping. She steps an inch backward. He crawls closer on his knee.

You saw their ad on TV the other day. I applied online.

When the woman stays silent, the man continues: *The Elvis impersonators, they give the big live performances that everyone loves. But only for men, they don't perform for women at all.*

OK, yeah, I remember. She blinks, trying to steady her quivering lower lip. As her face tries to betray the soggy, awful feeling tickling the back of her throat, she bites down on her lip, hard, with her front teeth.

Please, come with me to High Plains. We can both have a fresh start.

We can move in together, he adds.

Behind her nose, her confused tears freeze. She gawks at the television behind him, muted with no sound. There an Elvis in a white jumpsuit pirouettes and prances, lights gleaming on his bedazzled red jewels. Elvis's washboard abs glitter in the spotlight as he gyrates his hips.

Will you take your clothes off? she asks.

Not if you don't want me to. Are you coming?

Closing her eyes, she sees herself driving away from the house where she grew up. A house of noisy pipes, creaky floorboards, and silence.

She opens her eyes to find the man staring, brows crossed.

I've always had this fantasy, she says carefully. When her voice starts to wobble, she clears her throat.

Of me as Elvis?

Of a yellow house. A strong house with solid floors.

She stops.

Of living there . . . as a family, she continues.

Uh, well I'm sure they have yellow houses in High Plains. When he adjusts his gaze, his eyes are glazed. She sees the confusion float up to the surface of his eyes. She pictures him on the front porch of the yellow house, strumming his guitar while the purple tulips sway in the breeze. She sees them drinking coffee while years of their life pass: birthdays, anniversaries, holidays, all flick past her eyes in quick motion.

Keeping a straight face, the woman says very slowly, so she can control her voice: *OK, yes, I'll come to High Plains. Just give me a few weeks to research it.*

THE WOMAN MEETS HER AUNT AT HILDA'S. UNDER THE DIM LIGHTS AND STAINED CEILING, THEY DRINK COFFEE.

It looks like I'm about to go through another divorce, her aunt says as she rummages through her purse before lighting a long cigarette. *Do you have any money I could borrow? I'm not looking for much.*

Her aunt exhales a thick, aromatic cloud of smoke in the woman's face. The woman waves, trying to break up the smelly pall. A man in a suit enters the coffee shop with bird blood on his shoes, tracking blood on his path to the register.

The woman says quietly, *I've stopped job hunting.*

Do you plan to go back to school?

I don't think I'm going back. I'm moving to High Plains. He got a job at the All-Elvis enclave. We're moving in together. Eyes glistening, the woman searches her aunt's face.

Her aunt's beady pupils twitch; her brown eyes seem to tighten.

Didn't you just start dating?

I guess so.

Her aunt's face goes slack, then she adds quickly: *What does he think about your leaky boundaries?*

The woman's smile fades. *I haven't told him.*

You mean it hasn't just . . . happened? I thought it happened all the time?

I try not to let it happen when he's around.

If you move in together, how do you expect him not to find out? You know, it isn't everyone's cup of tea. Like has it ever . . . She points to her crotch. *Down there, during sex, does it ever . . .* She motions with her hands.

I don't understand.

Could it become a Venus flytrap and bite his dick off?

The woman doesn't say anything. Her expression freezes on her face.

I think most men would find that concept very frightening, her aunt adds.

Tears well in the woman's eyes. Not water from a nearby gutter; genuine human tears.

Of course not. How could you ask me something like that?

Sorry, didn't realize it was such a sensitive subject.

A hot pause.

Then in a lighter voice, her aunt adds, blowing another cloud of smoke in her face, *I'm sure he won't mind about your leaky boundaries. If it was him asking me to move, well, I would do the same if I were you.*

When she inhales, her lungs whistle. *I'm glad it's going so . . . well. My first boyfriend left me to join the circus.*

Right, the woman says, stunned. A single tear rolls down her face. The woman wipes it away before it trickles past her nose.

Anyways, I've got to get going. These lawyer checks won't write themselves, and unlike you, I don't have one of those Elvis impersonators as a boyfriend.

Her aunt tosses a five-dollar bill on the table, adjusts her faux-fur vest then prances out. Avoiding the blood prints with her soiled-cream stilettos.

The woman watches her leave through the smudged glass window. Instead of watching her red car retreat on the long road, the woman sighs, suddenly exhausted. She imagines the yellow house in High Plains. A yellow home with thick walls, sea breezes, and purple flowers in the yard. A home with a wraparound porch and a sturdy foundation.

The fantasy is accompanied by a tug at the bottom of her belly. A sinking or a lurch, hard to distinguish. The waitress approaches and asks if there is anything wrong. *The coffee's fine*, the woman says, *I think I am feeling a little sick.*

PART III

BEFORE BOARDING THE TRAIN TO HIGH PLAINS, NEVADA, THE WOMAN AND HER PURSE ARE SEARCHED.

She sleeps during the ride and wakes to the slur of wheels slowing.

From the window she absorbs High Plains, Nevada. A sky tinged with smoke. She counts the number of tall, black buildings, identical and faceless, until she reaches twenty-two. A turkey vulture lands on a streetlight next to the train window, the sun rippling on its black feathers.

At the arrivals platform, the man waits behind a barrier. His shoulders hunched near his ears. Moving toward him. She's clutching her potted plant from Pinecoast against her hip.

At the edge of the throng, their bodies connect. As she collapses into him, she says, *Home at last.*

Careening through the emptied station, he offers her a white handkerchief. *To protect your lips from the ash*, he says, forehead glossed with sweat.

Luggage in tow, they sprint toward the yellow cab gunning in the shade. Heat throttles her lungs.

Yellow cab smashing through strange, cool streets. The graffiti on the side of a concrete building reads, HIGH PLAINS, CITY OF HOMELESS COWS. She asks out loud, *Homeless cows?*

The cab driver says, *In High Plains, cows run free in the city. There is nowhere for them to graze. All the nearby pastures have caught fire.*

The taxi stops and the cabbie beeps his horn. In the street, a herd of cows exposing their slack, red tongues. The herd just stands in the middle of the street. Ribs poke out from their skin as they look out with lost, betrayed eyes. One brown cow gapes at the woman, its eyes glistening black.

The cabbie gets out of the taxi, kicking the brown cow in the rear—the herd splits, the scraping of their hooves against the street. As the taxi drives away, she peers out the rearview window, watching a white calf dodge a yellow school bus. The scrambling of cow hooves continues to pound inside her skull. As the cow feet strike the inside of her forehead, her head aches with the thundering pulse of their hooves. Long after the animals vanish.

You have any pain relievers on you? she asks.

Nope. What's up?

Nothing.

The scenery slips past the moving cab. The shadows of tall buildings of reflective black, streetlights, traffic, cows, absorbing the scene around her, she almost doesn't hear the taxi driver's voice when he speaks:

The air never used to be so thick. Charred debris from the wildfires, ash from the prison. My windshield wipers are just fast enough to keep the glass clear. Soon I will have to invest in stronger wipers. After that . . .

When she adjusts her position to stare at a vulture, the leather smacks as her damp skin unsticks from the seat. Staring at the vulture's dark feathers and pink talons, her thoughts begin to loop in concentric circles.

What if my feet become turkey vulture talons? What if I try to caress his face and end up scratching him with my claws? What if my touch scars his cheeks and he forces me to pay for plastic surgery?

This is us. The man dispenses a wad of cash into the cab driver's palm. Outside their new apartment complex, the woman widens her step to evade a cow snacking on a crow. She notes the complex is painted white, not yellow. There is no porch.

IN THE LOBBY OF THE POP'S COLA HOTEL, THE RECEPTIONIST SITS AT A DESK DECORATED WITH HEADLESS BARBIE DOLLS. THE WOMAN WAITS FOR HER INTERVIEW TO BEGIN.

The woman bursts into Mr. Boss's office while he is stacking a penny on top of a high copper stack. Pennies clatter to the glass desk. *Oh*, Mr. Boss says, trying to cover the splurged mess with his elbows.

She settles into a plastic POP'S COLA chair opposite him. Scent of hand sanitizer. Mr. Boss raps his knuckles on his desk. He says, *Welcome to the COLA Hotel, please sit.* The woman freezes. She is already sitting.

The aquarium on the left wall, filled with Siamese fighting fish, feels like a disaster waiting to happen.

Let me clarify the expectations of the position: you'd be more than just a cleaner, he says, fingering a penny and dropping it on his desk. *Guests from around the world visit our hotels. To them, you represent soda.*

She points her head down at her sandals, her toes decorated

with the scales of the fish in the tank. She curls her toes, trying to hide the glinting scales on her feet. Magenta, square, catching the light.

I'm a selfish worker, she says, keeping her voice quiet, meek, her eyes now fixed on his chin.

Selfless, she stumbles, *I meant to say selfless.*

I see. He hesitates, running his thumb across a stack of papers. After an extended pause, he says quietly, *You're hired*, and lobs the papers across the desk. She catches the contract with her right hand. *But I can only pay you the minimum wage. COLA standard. Hope you understand.*

That's fine.

Mr. Boss stands, *There is something a little . . . strange about you. Really. But I am not one to refuse someone for living outside the so-called box. However, the product is paramount. I want the COLA hotel rooms to radiate and dazzle.*

Mr. Boss reclines fully in his desk chair. Outside the office window, a child screams as he cannonballs into the outdoor pool. A maid hurries around the deck, placing soda cans into a garbage bag.

The woman turns her attention to the contract. On the page, the letters leap out from the words, twisting free of their boundaries. She squints her eyes, then massages her temple with her fingertips, but nothing changes.

The skin of his pen is cool in her hands.

Finding the dotted line, signing it.

THE WOMAN GETS HOME BREATHLESS. NOT NOTICING HER RED CHEEKS, THE MAN ASKS THE WOMAN TO POSE FOR A PHOTOGRAPH. LET'S SEE YOU IN YOUR NEW UNIFORM, HE SAYS.

It's a POP'S COLA hotel? he asks in a voice tight like a wire.

Yes, she says, spinning for him, off balance, she catches the floor with her foot. The light splashes on her COLA uniform—its logo embellished in pink cursive.

I told you I was interviewing, she says. *I thought that's why you bought me a soda yesterday.*

That was just a coincidence, he says, *I didn't know it was a COLA hotel.* His whole body sags as if a hard wind had pressed all the energy out of him.

Her cheeks humiliated red, legs wobbly: *I walked all over. They were the only place hiring.*

Straightening, he grips his camera. *Take it off.*

What?

Take off your uniform.

She removes the white dress with the POP'S COLA logo. Putting her hand on the meat of her hip. Her lips search for expression. Sweat grows down her temples. Nipples hard in the air-conditioning.

Click, click, click.

She tries to smile, suck in her stomach, and flex her legs. Placing her hand on her hip to make her arms look slim. She grins, pouts, and straightens her face. But the man takes too long, takes too many pictures. She gives up, slouching, as she sucks her lower lip. Her body begins to tremble, feeling the chilly air tingle against her legs.

I'm cold, she offers.

Fine. We can stop.

She flops on the couch, wrapping herself in a fleece blanket. Once covered up, she lets out a long exhale through her mouth. *I'm exhausted*, she says. Mouth twisted, she chews the inside of her cheek.

From taking a picture? he says, fixated on his camera screen as he reviews the photos.

She tries to say something to him, but his replies are mute, nonplussed. He shuts off the camera. *I'm going to the Elvis enclave to write*, he says, slipping inside his coat.

After the door shuts, she paces the living room for twenty minutes

before flicking on the television. Soothed. Though she barely listens

and the meteorologist is such a drag.

ON HER FIRST DAY OF WORK, THE WOMAN KNEELS IN FRONT OF A HUMAN-SIZE SCULPTURE OF A COLA BOTTLE.

At the front of the room, Mr. Boss commands, *Scrub, my beauteous army, scrub.* The sound of women furiously scouring. Glass sculptures of COLA bottles. Populating the hotel lobby.

The woman's arms ache. Swiping ash flecks from the COLA bottle's neck. *Let our sculptures glisten*, Mr. Boss says. He pens a box on his clipboard.

Her sponge passes over the COLA sculpture's curvaceous waist. Next, she scrubs an ash patch off the breast just before it swivels into its neck. As the woman squeezes her sponge, her bucket of foam grows darker. She grips the sponge again, seeing the black bubbles pour over her hand.

She remembers Momma's black lips through the prison fence; the members of the blue-uniforms trudging past her in the entryway of the house—a water gurgles in her stomach, threatens to burst out her mouth. She swipes her sponge, hard, almost cutting the corner against the sculpture's glass hip.

Mr. Boss looms behind her. Hears the spectacle of his voice in her ear. Doesn't process the meaning of his words, only their hard, bright shapes. She concentrates on the ground beneath her sneakers. Mr. Boss returns to the center of the room, scribbling on his clipboard.

What did he just say? she asks the brunette next to her.

No idea, the brunette says.

Thanks.

The woman and the brunette pause to watch a commercial play on the lobby TV. On the screen, a group of dancing Elvis impersonators. The man appears on the TV, wearing a white jumpsuit decorated with red gems, feverishly shaking his hips.

That's him, the woman points at the TV, *that's my boyfriend.*

That's your boyfriend? the brunette asks.

Yep. We live together.

What's it like living with an Elvis?

He's always working.

Typical.

Then the brunette adds: *Hey, what's that on your neck?*

A patch of cow fur has appeared at the place where the woman's spine meets her skull. A circle of fur, the size of a dime, on the nape of her neck.

I was petting a cow earlier, the woman's voice cracks, *I've got to wash off later.*

I see.

The woman freezes until the ad finishes. Then she turns to say something, a shallow remark, but the brunette isn't there; she must be refreshing the cleaning solution in the supply closet. She finishes wiping down the sculpture and heads to the hotel room at the start of the hall.

Removing a used condom from the floor, scrubbing the sink and toilet bowl with bleach, holding her breath in a room that smells like there's something rotting inside. She tries to discover the source by looking under the bed. Searches the drawers. Opens a window.

Finally, she sees the outline of a bird in the trash can. A seagull, its white feathers matted with oil and gray-black ash. The smell of rot and gasoline, thick in her nostrils like smog. Holding her breath, she hoists the bag out of the can. Maybe, she thinks, someone planned to burn the bird at one point but forgot to strike the match.

Holding the bag away from her nose, she carries the dead bird to the dumpster, then heads to the bathroom to wash her hands. Holding her breath. Hearing nothing aside from her sneakers hitting the cold concrete. Tap, tap, tap.

If it were possible to be less than a person, if it were possible to be nothing at all.

In the bathroom, she scours her hands with soap three times over, but the putrid smell lingers on her fingers. She retreats into the bathroom stall. There she takes a minute to steady her shaking hands by placing them on her thighs. Then there's the squeak of the bathroom door opening, the sliding of sneakers against ceramic tile. Instinctively, she tucks her feet into a fetal position, so no one will know she's there.

What a freak show, one of the women says. The woman recognizes the voice of the brunette worker she'd chatted with earlier.

Do you see the way Mr. Boss talks to her? the woman doesn't recognize the second female voice.

Yeah. Like she doesn't speak English.

You know her mom's the professor they said killed all those birds, the brunette says. *Like ten years ago. Her face was all over the news.*

No shit.

Look at this picture. She looks just like her. That's why she won't tell anyone her name.

The woman hears their footsteps strike the tile as the ladies get close.

You're right. They do look alike. That's fucking hysterical.

Oh yeah. Crazy runs in the family.

They begin to imitate the squawking of dying seagulls: a high-pitched scrape from the back of their throats. Their fake cawing followed by loud chuckling. The woman hugs her knees closer to her chest, listening to their laughter rise toward the ceiling as their conversation drifts to other subjects.

Do you smell that? the brunette says.

Smells like something died in the walls.

Classic.

Taps running, dripping, their sneakers scuffing the tile as they walk out. Then silence. The woman unfolds her body, loose and humiliated, and exits the stall. She approaches the mirror, staring at her reflection for several minutes. In the glass, she tries to find Momma's nose, Momma's eyes, Momma's bone structure. But her image wiggles back in the glass: absent, blank, blinking.

THE NEXT MORNING, THE WOMAN WAKES UP ALONE. TWO STORIES BELOW, THE WOMAN WATCHES COWS CRAWL INTO THE STREET.

A brown cow crosses the street. Then an oil-colored car approaches. Pausing, the car blares its horn. The brown cow freezes in the middle of the street. The oil-colored car honks again: no response.

So the car pushes forward, hitting the cow in the flank. Instead of capering off, the animal stands there. As the car moves forward, the animal sinks: its front legs collapse, its hind legs fall, bending its head downward. As the car continues to inch and inch and inch, slowly, treading across the cow's neck, snapping its hips, crushing its femur, pressing its ribs flat into the pavement. A pressed flower.

As bones crack and joints pop, the cow's hide begins to split at the neck and flank. For a long moment, the sharp crackling of the body fills the air. The cow moans, its cry sharp like a blade. As the car finishes riding its body like a wave.

The car returns to the pavement. Leaving the cow in the road, its eyes black as stars. The car doesn't stop to apprehend the damage; it continues forward, tires treading blood into the pavement for half a block.

The woman waits but doesn't feel the cow's moan bubbling in her own throat. Today she is protected by the window glass. Apprehending the dead cow in the street. The cool buzz of the air-conditioning. The cool, artificial air releases itself from the ceiling slits and wafts across her bare feet and legs, sneaking up the window of her nightgown.

Kicking one of the man's Elvis wigs underneath the bedframe, the woman lies across their unmade bed. Resting her limbs among the soft sheets. Closing her eyes. Trying to forget the searing wail of the cow. Listening to the city breathe outside the apartment: honking cars and garbage trucks, pedestrians, the clobbering of cow hooves.

The jolt of the front door opening shakes her into a sitting position.

The man in the doorway of the studio, his white jumpsuit unzipped. *Hey.* He perches at the little table and scrapes off his wig. Drumming his finger on the table, not saying anything. *Did you have a bad night, Elvis?* she asks. He continues to stare out the window, silent.

Why didn't you come home last night? she interjects into the silence.

He puts his head into his forearms. *We practiced all night. So I didn't get any sleep. I had an accident on my way home.*

Do you want to talk about it?

In the middle of the street, the cow floods the street with blood. Pedestrians hobble around the blood pooling in the gutter.

No, he says. *What time will you be home from work tomorrow?*

Eight o'clock, she says. *It's a double shift.*

He says, *I don't understand you. Why would you work for a company responsible for imprisoning your mother?*

Feeling all her tired insides lurch inside her stomach. Feeling the man's eyes watching her.

What are those spikes? the man says, looking at her forearm.

Oh, the woman looks down at the black fur of the potted plant on both her arms. *I just . . . need to shave.*

I didn't know girls shaved their arms.

Yeah.

The man looks at her dead in the eye. He sighs and begins to talk. Her shoulders relax down her back as she smiles and nods. Not listening, the woman looks down at the floorboards and imagines her feet sinking into the maple. She sees herself, abandoned and stagnant, as the world around her rots.

Are you listening? the man says. She shakes her head up and down.

He continues: *To call POP'S COLA "evil" undercuts the spread of their harm. You know none of the higher-ups live within one hundred miles of a prison. Over time, ordinary humans will begin to feel the effects of what we've been inhaling. Not just birds and prisoners. As usual, it will impact our most vulnerable. People of color, women, the poor.*

In her mind, the woman pictures Momma's wide eyes the day of their last visit, hours before the woman boarded the train. How Momma said nothing when the woman told her she was leaving. Momma had just looked at her, eyes wild, her gray hair floating around her ash-stained face. The woman had been afraid to look back when she strode to the exit.

The memory causes a shudder to hammer up the woman's spine, seep through her neck muscles, and drip into her brain.

I couldn't find work anywhere else, she says, hearing her voice distantly, as if from far away.

He just stares at her.

They own a third of this city, she continues.

Don't make excuses. Take responsibility. That's the problem with people these days, nobody wants . . .

Instead of replying, she leaps up, flying out the apartment so quickly the hem of her miniskirt flips up, exposing her thighs.

She stops in the hallway of their shared complex, pressing her back against the wall. Breathing in small, imperfect gulps. Tries to ignore that feeling in her belly, wild and sickening to perceive, making her head feel topsy-turvy. A cold sweat breaks out down her spine. Outside, a cow whimpers.

THE MAN ASKS THE WOMAN TO TUNE INTO HIS RADIO INTERVIEW, SO SHE DOWNLOADS THE SHOW ONTO HER LAPTOP.

Interviewer: *Thank you, Elvis #2225, for coming here to talk with us at 100.3 Pirate Radio FM. We want to know: what inspires your art?*

Man: *Like a battery, I get charged by the pervasive violence of the natural earth as well as the government's refusal to act properly. To name the real enemy, you could say. My creative glands get so tickled by all of this, I start to salivate all over the page.*

Interviewer: *What concerns you most about our government's handling of the climate crisis?*

Man: *Our government is more concerned with the profits of corporations like POP'S COLA than the livelihood of its citizens.*

Many of us feel broken and defeated by the awareness of the corruption that surrounds us, yet we feel powerless to alter our situation. At this moment, our system is unable to manifest the energy to rehabilitate itself.

Interviewer: *So how do you find pleasure in times as grim as these?*

Man: *Well, I am someone who has lost much. So pleasure has always been fickle or fleeting, I guess.*

Interviewer: *But you manage to come by it?*

Man: *I've never been good at maintaining a relationship with myself or with pleasure. But I am most fulfilled when I am Elvis: in tight leather pants, shaking my hips on the stage, hearing my lyrics reach a receptive, all-male audience. In this position I've found the most freedom. But I suppose because I am pretending to be someone, my pleasure is artificial.*

Interviewer: *Do you think there is such thing as "genuine pleasure"?*

Man: *Yes, but it is in danger of going extinct.*

Interviewer: *Please explain.*

Man: *Well, when I am walking down the shoal of a fake beach, the breeze that strikes my face is generated by a motored fan. It's not real. The sand beneath my boots: it's plastic, as fake as sitcom dialogue or friends on social media. And this is the direction we are heading in if we don't attempt to mend our habits. There will be no real pleasure left: no sea to ride, no green curve in the hills. When no natural world remains, all pleasure will be virtual.*

Interviewer: *Would you like a tissue?*

Man: *No, no, those aren't real tears: I've developed an allergy to my Elvis wig.*

Interviewer: *Well, we are so grateful to speak with you, and we want to mention that you are presently dressed as "Jailhouse Rock" Elvis in our basement studio today.*

Man: *Uh, thank you, thank you very much.*

TWO NIGHTS AND THE MAN DOES NOT COME HOME. ON THE SECOND NIGHT, SHE SLIPS OUT THE DOOR OF THEIR NEW APARTMENT. SHE CATCHES A YELLOW CAB AND RIDES IT TO THE ALL-ELVIS ENCLAVE.

NO WOMEN ALLOWED, a sign tacked to the fence reads.

In front of the chain-link fence, she digs a hole in the sand, careful not to alert the sleeping guard in a plastic chair on one side of the locked gate. Before sliding under the fence, she casts another glance at the guard, his chin snoozing on his chest.

She imagines the guard waking up from his sleep, her having to explain she's on a mission to find her lost boyfriend. *He's been gone for two days, officer*, she says out loud to the desert.

As she shimmies her belly under the barbs, she tries to avoid pricking her leg on a cactus. On the other side of the fence, she breathes cleanly. Then picks up the pace, sliding a little in the sand, as the guard's snoring grows faint behind her, her pulse drumming in her ears.

She capers through the sandy courtyard illuminated with solar lamps and statues of Elvis. The conical solar lamps beam their yellow glances onto the statues and sand. Thundering across the dark courtyard, she passes stone statues of Elvis in various positions. Praying Elvis. Thoughtful Elvis. Elvis in a lei. There is even a statue of Elvis on his wedding day, posed next to Priscilla in her pearled dress.

She searches the darkness beyond the lamps and statues, but there is no one around.

The woman is drawn like a spider to the sound of drumbeats coming from the long wood building where lights blaze in square windows. As she pictures the man, in a chamber, being tortured by a bevy of whip-bearing Elvis impersonators, she starts to sprint.

What if he never comes home? What if I die in the apartment choking on an apple and there is no one to discover my body? What if they don't discover me until I'm badly decomposed, and, at my funeral, everyone talks about how bad my corpse smelled?

It takes her four minutes to reach the building. She steps through the back entrance. From the lighted stage, the music pours out like holy water. Facing the stage, a crowd of at least two hundred men: sitting in plastic chairs, their eyes drawn in worship to the performance.

She searches the room for the man but doesn't see him.

On the stage, two dudes in black poufed wigs, dancing. Both wear white Elvis jumpsuits as they sing to the tune of "Hound

Dog." One guy shakes his hips and moves closer to the other. Together, they grind their hips against each other. Their chests shine as if greased with oil. One Elvis thrusts his crotch against the other Elvis's thigh.

Men in the front row jump to their feet, frantically clapping, shouting. *Elvis, Elvis*, they cry. The woman stands at the back of the audience, silent and unseen. She doesn't see the man anywhere, though her searching eyes continue to rove.

> *You ain't nothing but a seagull*
> *Dying all the time*

One Elvis unzips his jumpsuit, exposing his bare torso.

The crowd roars.

The other Elvis unzips his jumpsuit down to his right ankle, sheds the suit and steps out of the clothing, nude. The woman avoids looking at the stage and glares down at her shoes. The crowd is now, basically, all on their feet. The jeering, clapping, and shouting overwhelm the room.

Finally, she looks up and sees the Elvis impersonator, naked, lathered in a glittering oil. His washboard abs reflect the spotlight. His jumpsuit in a pile on the stage, he shakes his waist to the beat of the song. She tries to focus on his face and ignore his naked, swaying hips.

The woman scurries out through the back door, aimless and marching around the Elvis courtyard. The quiet of the yard cut by the hard stomp of her sandals on sand. Creeping under the solar lamps, the shadows of Elvis statues.

Standing on her tip toes and peering inside, she searches the lit windows of eight cabins. But though she sees an Elvis passed out, naked, a bottle in his hand, in the front room, the woman doesn't spy the man. Beyond the cabins and the venue and the courtyard, the silence is black and crackling. Where is he?

She crosses the courtyard back to the entrance, where she squiggles under the chain-link fence. At his watch, the guard snores in his chair. Creeping past him, the woman hides behind a cactus one hundred feet from the entrance. She checks her watch: 9:13 p.m. How long will she have to wait?

In the darkness beyond her, the hot bugs croon. The snakes slither and creep. The moon is a solar lamp, beaming onto the statue of the woman.

Twenty minutes later, the man steps out of the enclave through the guarded gate. Dressed in a tan GI uniform, his black wig streaked flat on his forehead. The guard, now awake, checks his papers and lets him pass through.

The woman steps out from behind the cactus. Squinting, the man raises his forearm in greeting. His black wig slides forward and he adjusts it with his hand. On the shoulder of his tan GI uniform, a tuft of black ash trembles. As he moves toward her, the breeze scoops the large ash flake off his shoulder and it disappears into the night.

You're here, he says.

She tiptoes closer to him, her hands clutching her biceps. Her glassy eyes reflect the bright lights of the enclave as her mind replays the image of the Elvis impersonator wiggling his booty and swinging his genitals. The woman gulps. Sorry, she says to herself, I didn't intend to see another man's junk tonight.

It's been two days since I've seen you, she says to the man. *I worried something happened.*

I guess I lost track of time, the man shrugs. *I'm sorry. Let's go, I know where to catch a cab.*

He grabs her wrist. They walk down a sand path toward the road where yellow headlights slice the night open. The man raises his arm. A neon cab swerves to the side of the road, kicking up palls of sand as it skids to a stop.

In the moving yellow cab, her voice falls across the leather seat. *Where have you been?* she says. *You've been gone for days.*

The Elvises were practicing the musical I wrote. I was rewriting the lyrics in my cabin. He stares out at the passing lights.

She says, *Do you take your clothes off when you perform?*

Of course not, he replies. *But no women allowed, remember?* His voice soft. Against his tan uniform, his eyes look darker. She's aware of the leather seat separating them; headlights from a passing cab are piercing white.

You didn't watch any of the performances tonight, did you?

Of course not. When she swallows, she feels like she's choking on glass.

Good girl, he pats the top of her head.

Reaching across the space, she puts her hand on top of his. He inches closer to her.

By the way, I've decided I want you to call me by my new name, he adds. *The King.*

Her eyes, gleaming in fear, connect with his own. She recognizes no one in them, just pure, unadulterated blue, marred by a spot of black. As the image of the naked, dancing Elvis plays and replays over and over in her mind, she looks down at her free hand, trembling against the taxi seat.

As the scenery changes from darkness and shrubs to city skyscrapers and streetlights. The silence drifts and flakes between them. Her thoughts seize and twist. She clenches her teeth.

She starts to count the number of skyscrapers they pass, immediately starting over once she reaches twenty. Twenty was a safe number, easy to multiply, divide, and put back together. Twenty was a safe number unlike the man's eyes.

THE FOLLOWING WEEK, THE MAN GETS BACK LATE TO THE APARTMENT. THEY GO TO A PATIO BAR WITH POTTED PLANTS HANGING FROM THE CEILING, WHERE MIST STREAMS OUT OF LITTLE MACHINES.

A little mist all over her skin and hair. Drinks of vodka and water. A little sip. A little bite of her green salad.

The man studies his binder full of Elvis song lyrics. Hardly touching his vegan sandwich: tofu and spinach pressed between slices of focaccia. Plate dotted with spots of yellow mustard. The woman inquires if he'd like to order dessert. He sings his reply: *I'm all shook up.*

Why are you singing? she asks.

> *Please don't ask me what's on my mind,*
> *I'm a little shook up but I'm feeling fine*

Do you want dessert?

In a flat tone, he says, *You shouldn't be eating so much. That's something we talk about at the enclave.*

My appetite?

No. Women's habits. A cockroach slithers up the spine of a potted fig tree. Pausing for a moment, its tentacles touching the green leaf.

What do you mean? she says, feeling cockroach legs tickle the lining of her stomach. Instinctively she grabs her stomach, preparing to vomit. But her fingers stay human, her legs don't morph: the body holds.

The other day an Elvis told me about a scientific paper he saw online. The paper suggested the presence of an enzyme caused some mice to snack more. The scientists claimed our genetic differences may impact our tendencies for environmental harm. Not to say I agree with this idea entirely, he says, sipping his water, *I think some women turn to food—to fill their voids—which makes excess waste.*

She flaps her lips as the man lifts a spinach leaf from his plate.

I hate that feeling.

What feeling? he says, inspecting the limp blade closely, his lips tucked in disgust. He flings the wilted spinach leaf to the floor.

Blame.

I think you mean shame, which is a response to blame. If you don't do anything wrong, there's no reason to feel shame.

When she doesn't respond, he returns to the song lyrics in his binder. Humming the tune of "All Shook Up." Tapping his heel against the barstool.

She takes one last bite of her salad then stops. As she pushes her plate away, she notices an ash flake on the rim of her white plate. She reaches out, smudges it with her finger, which smears the black streak across the lip of the plate. She raises her hand for the waiter's attention; he removes the plate in a hurry. Listening to the whirring of the ceiling fans above her. Artificial mist. Bar music.

She doesn't process the feeling—of the man's blame—until that night. In bed next to her, the man snores under the lamplight of the moon. Hearing his breaths rise and fall.

Pinching the edge of her tongue beneath her teeth, she remembers the day the blue-uniforms came for Momma. Standing in the doorway, peering at them through the window: how their faces had looked trustworthy. Their copper wires swung from their belts, shining in the ebbing light. Pulling the front door open. Suddenly the blue-uniforms were there, big and tall, like trees. She had stepped back from the doorway, then melted into the wall, flat. The tap-tap-tap of their black boots as they trampled through the threshold.

Listening to the man's huddled breath, the moonlight spilling in from the window. She can't find the smooth spot of sleep, so her legs tangle and thrash in the sheets. She imagines the door bursting open: a brown cow pinning her to the floor before slicing her throat with a spork. She sees her blood pouring through the slit in her neck, blood bubbling up through her lips. *They were trying to get their revenge*, she whispers into the room, *for what I've allowed to happen*. But the man doesn't hear the woman, at least, she doesn't see him wake up.

THE MAN TEXTS THE WOMAN TO MEET HIM AT THE RESTAURANT AFTER HIS SHIFT. HE'S HALF AN HOUR LATE, BUT HE SHOWS UP.

In the center of the street, a cow with its organs spilling out of its mouth. A shroud of flies buzzes around its flat torso. The cow's sooty-gray liver and yellow intestines pushed out of its broken jaw.

Look, the man says, pointing.

Perched on the cow's spine, a troop of large blackbirds with orange feet. Their shined feathers and dark beaks. The birds peck at the cow's entrails: white tubular chunks soaked in blood. The birds flick strips of white meat onto the sidewalk as they feed. Swallowing a piece of intestine, one blackbird spreads its wings wide. The sunlight cascades on its jet-black feathers.

The woman imagines herself in the middle of the road, the man eating her intestines with a spork. Not alive, not dead. The fly wings humming like machines in her ears, the birds pecking and feasting on her with blood-soaked beaks.

You should have changed after work, the man's voice thunders in her ears. He points at the POP'S COLA logo near the hem of her white uniform.

Take my blazer, he begins to remove his coat, *to cover the POP'S logo*.

He shoves the blazer in her direction, roughly grazing her knuckles as she extends her arms to accept it. Sliding her hands through the sleeves, she says, *Are you embarrassed by me?*

Shh, the man says, laying his finger across her lips. *It's my fans I'm thinking of.*

She bites her lip, pressing its fat between her teeth.

She follows him into the restaurant foyer. Under the slick, artificial light, his eyes turn soft as he chats with the hostess. The hostess bats her long eyelashes, *Right this way Mr. Elvis.* She sits them at opposite ends of a diamond-shaped table. From the waitress, the man orders a cooked goose for them to share.

Eventually the cooked goose arrives on an iron plate, sizzling. He lifts it to his lips and begins to eat with his hands. Drops of fat fall from his lips. A feather gets lodged between his teeth. The woman refuses to take a bite, claiming she's not hungry.

The man begins to chatter about how the government is intertwined with corporate power, how political involvement is the highest type of moral act. As he talks, she notices a clear liquid swimming in his eyes. Reflecting the light, the liquid smears his black pupils. For a second his blue eyes shine gray. Or are they green?

She thinks: I can't see inside of you.

When she reaches for her water, the last thing she senses is the chilly glass around her palm. The scene before her briefly flashes white—the table, the cooked goose, the man's dark wig. She wakes on the floor of the restaurant with the man's face hovering above her own. His face is not one of concern, necessarily. He's smiling, almost pleased, she closes her eyes, somewhere between falling asleep and waking up.

The last thing she remembers is trying to control her boundaries. Then seeing his grin, slightly menacing, float up behind her closed lids.

LEAVING THE COLA HOTEL, THE WOMAN SEES HER AUNT ON THE SIDEWALK, GRIPPING A LEOPARD-PRINT SUITCASE.

Sweetie, her aunt says, wrapping her arms around the woman. *Ew, you're all sweaty.* She recoils.

I've just finished work.

I know you have. Look who came to surprise you. Her aunt places her hands on her hips and puckers her red lips, lipstick smeared outside the lines. Then she adds quickly: *Please don't tell anyone you've seen me.*

Why?

She pauses. *I may have gotten myself into a bit of trouble over a silly purse. I didn't think it would be too big of a deal. To just take it. But you know how uptight those corporations are, all about making a buck.*

A particle of ash spindles from the sky, finally nesting in her aunt's hair. The woman flicks it gently with her index finger, then grabs her aunt's suitcase. Its suede handle feels plush and warm. The sunlight, firm on her back. She fixes her mouth into a smile.

Well, I'm glad you came. Sorry you're in a bit of trouble. How long are you here for?

Less than twelve hours.

What do you want to do?

Go to the casino of course, I've heard their fake beach is much better than the one in Pinecoast. I've got a wig in my suitcase. I'll slap it on and we'll be on our way.

At the fake beach, the waitress delivers two Bloody Marys on a shaking tray. Across the table, her aunt is in costume: a shapeless black frock, combat boots, and a blonde wig. Tufts of red hair stick out from her lopsided bob wig, which bulges near her ear.

Within thirty seconds, her aunt drains her Bloody Mary. She slurps the red juice from the ice cubes with her straw, then starts to gnaw on her celery stick. Looking around and keeping her voice low, her aunt says, *I heard a rumor about your boyfriend.*

Really?

He used to have a different girlfriend. A backup singer in his band. She was a fake blonde with bad skin. They were together for a while, then no one saw her around anymore.

You must be thinking of someone else.

Honey, a man who sings about bird sex is unforgettable.

Well, he's mentioned none of this to me. And I've never heard him sing about sex with animals.

I'm just telling you what I know. Bertha's the hairdresser at Locks so she hears a lot . . . she stops to suck the dregs of her cocktail through her straw.

He asked me to move here with him. The woman can hear her voice start to quiver. *Even if it is true, whatever happened with her won't happen with me.*

Unless your Venus flytrap vag eats his ding-dong.

Please don't joke about that.

Seriously, have you given him the 411 on your boundaries?

The woman shakes her head.

Her aunt uses her index finger to make a circle around the woman. *This is a disaster in waiting. Here's an idea. Get ahead of the scandal. Just tell him, hey, sometimes the outside world . . .* she changes her voice an octave, so it's low and smooth . . . *slips inside me. Say it just like I did just then.*

Her aunt shrugs, switching her voice back. *Maybe he'll find it kind of hot. Men are freaks like that.*

She slurps the last traces of her drink loudly with her straw.

The bottom line is, you two are already living together. Breakups are harder when you cohabitate. He's less likely to cut it off now that you share a bed.

The woman feels her fingernails harden. *I can't.*

Well . . . if you keep this a secret, it might all blow up in your face. And trust me, I know a lot about blowing things up.

Her aunt grins, widening her eyes emphatically. *You seem stressed. Do you want me to buy you another Bloody Mary?*

I'm fine. What else do you want to do at the casino? the woman continues.

Slots. Then I've got to hit the road.

Maybe we could play together?

That would be nice. We couldn't do this type of stuff when you were young. Hurry up and finish your drink. I've got a bag of coins in my purse, you can have some. Are you ready to bingo, bitch?

The woman follows, listening to the throaty satin of her aunt's voice babbling about her ex as they enter the casino floor.

AFTER WORK, THE WOMAN ENTERS THE APARTMENT, WHERE THE MAN IS DRAPED ACROSS THE LOVE SEAT. SPREAD ACROSS THE FLAT SCREEN: A SKYSCRAPER COLLAPSING.

What movie are you watching? she asks.

No answer.

Sliding onto the love seat, she asks, *Is that skyscraper really falling?* On the screen, a black building tumbles into the ground, eroding into a fan of black dust. Within thirty seconds, the building lies flattened on the sidewalk. Staring at the screen, she waits for the what-if questions to ramp up. Instead, nothing happens.

He smirks, *It's pretty clear what's happening.*

Well, I don't feel anything. She remembers the pamphlet about the birds, how they fly around the world only to find themselves at the beginning. Lightheaded, she lets her chin rest in her palms.

The newscaster's voice: *This morning, temperatures in San Angelo rose so high, the steel bearings of its tallest skyscraper melted. The building collapsed just after two p.m., the hottest hour of the day. Three people were estimated to be inside the building when it fell.*

This is a disgrace, the news anchor continues, *the State has failed us. We have been humiliated on an international stage. We hope the people involved with permitting this building will be held . . .*

Responsible. The woman finishes the news anchor's sentence. She sinks deeper into the couch, hearing cars bloom on the street. An ambulance barrels past the apartment, its siren making red colors.

The woman turns to the man: *On the way to work yesterday, I saw a sign that said POP'S COLA was finding ways to profit off environmental chaos.*

You don't know what you are talking about, he says, *I've been studying this stuff for years.*

She starts, *I thought–*

The man's hand hits the edge of her mouth first, then strikes her cheek. The taste of his fingers is sharp.

The red imprint of his hand stains her cheek. She touches her shocked mouth with her hand and then scrutinizes her fingers. Frail, small fingers. Tiny like the rib bones of a bird.

Confused, she tries to speak but ends up biting down on her own tongue. Little tears sprout in her eyes, but she holds them back. In her mind, she pictures the man bleeding from his crotch, screaming bloody murder because her Venus flytrap vagina has bitten off his penis.

Huffing, the man is upright. Stomping into the kitchen. Returning to the love seat with an ice-cream cone, over-flowing. His pink lips parting. He crams the cone into his mouth.

Sorry, he says, noticing her shocked face. *But you shouldn't act like I don't know what I am talking about.*

Silence, inches between them, like invisible pores opening in heat. She touches her cheek with her hand as the pain roars on her flesh. Her voice catches in her throat.

Her eyes fix on the strawberry ice-cream cone in his hands. His fat, pink tongue licking the cone indiscriminately. She spits out the first sentence that enters her mind.

You're just as bad as I am.

He licks the bubble gum–colored cone again.

To the environment. If you're eating that ice-cream cone, she continues, *you're just as bad as me or anyone else.*

Her comment hangs in the air between them like a veil of smoke. She focuses on the potted plant near the window. Its green leaves tremble as an airplane thunders across the sky, briefly shaking the little black table.

On the couch, the man stops chewing. For a second, he holds the ice cream in his mouth. His eyes spin wildly around the room. Then he spits out the half-chewed cone from his mouth and into his hands. As a final gesture, he spews out a spoonful of pink drool, his saliva tinged with melted cream.

In his hand, a mound of ice cream guts. Masticated, pink cream, shreds of the soggy cone, red strawberry flecks, and a pool of his saliva. Cheeks steaming, his face bent toward his hands. A drop of pink cream slides from between his cupped fingers, hitting the wood.

I need to eat. His voice is velvet, tender.

Another glob of pink cream leaks out from his palms.

The man gets up, leaving a trail of pink droplets from the couch to the counter. The woman stiffens. He throws the melted pink cream and the masticated cone in the trash can. The woman hears the faucet flowing, the dish soap bubbling as he works it into a lather between his palms. Then the man looms by the counter for a moment. He doesn't approach. Resting both hands on the granite, glaring at her.

The silence expands like a spider's web. Beat by beat, the silence crawls into her ears and lays eggs there. Could the silence result in her premature death? If her boundaries leaked and only the silence came inside her? Would her body explode? Guts and blood and bone? All over the man's face in messy splatters?

Pressing her nails into her fleshy palm, creating little incisions.

The man retreats into the bathroom and locks the door. Within minutes, she can hear the shower running and the sound of the man singing "Hound Dog." An ambulance passes five stories below. A loud, high-pitched whine fills the room, which reminds the woman of her childhood. The shower stops running, but the man does not emerge from the bathroom.

Blackness slaps all the windows. She draws the shades then leaves the apartment.

She eats dinner in solitude at a nearby diner. The siren from the passing ambulance continues to blare in her head while she eats her omelet. Hours of stunned silence pass. Staring out the diner at the happy couples completing their after-dinner strolls. The siren stays whirring in her head as she drags her sneakers back to the apartment.

She enters their apartment, the furniture shrouded in darkness. The moon, yellow and round, illuminates the bed, where the man draws the long breaths of sleep. As her eyes adjust to the dark, she notices a shape on the counter, which makes her shoulders jump.

Stepping forward, she smells a dampness, a whiff of rose. Stretching her hands forward in the dark, first her fingers graze something cold. A glass vase. She grips it from the counter and moves it close to her face. The loose, soft perfume of roses, their fingers brushing her cheeks.

She moves the vase into the light of the moon, where she sees a bouquet of twelve roses, gorgeous and full, carefully arranged in a vase. The light drips across their yellow, open petals. In the middle of the roses lies a card in an envelope. She opens it and reads a note from the man scrawled in pencil:

> *A bouquet of yellow flowers–to anticipate our years in the yellow house.*
>
> *I'm sorry–*

She puts the note back in the envelope and hoists the roses close to her nose. The smell hits her brain like a drug. Drawing long, unsteady breaths.

ON SUNDAY, TWO GROUPS OF PROTESTORS GATHER ON THE STREET BELOW THEIR APARTMENT. WHAT IS GOING ON OUT THERE, THE WOMAN ASKS THE MAN. I WOULDN'T GO FIND OUT, HE SAYS, BUT THE WOMAN HAS ALREADY STARTED FOR THE DOOR.

COLA + GOVERNMENT = TRUE LOVE, one protestor's sign reads. WE LOVE PROPAGANDA, another poster reads. Frowns and signs and clicking of cell phone keypads. A crowd of about thirty people melting under the hot sun.

Toward the back, the woman sees a gaggle of five protestors detached from the crowd. When they notice a cow bleeding in the shade nearby, the protestors whip out their cell phones and start to film it.

The white cow lays on the ground beneath a tented overhang, its pink tongue wagging out of its mouth. A pool of blood streams out from a wound on its flank; the cow pants as blood pours from its leg and sweat pours from its ears. The protestors shout slurs as they record it with their phones. One protestor kicks one of the cow's legs and they all chuckle.

A vulture approaches. The protestors gasp. The black vulture hobbles over to the puddle of blood. Ignoring the cow, the vulture lays down. Its red beak opens with delight as it spreads its wings and shimmies its body against the pavement. Its feathers soak up the blood on the sidewalk. The vulture lies there, motionless, for a long moment. The protestors are silent.

Finally, the vulture rises. Torrents of blood flow down its wingspan. The vulture spreads and shakes its dark wings as droplets of blood fly off the bird, showering the protestors' faces, arms, and legs.

Shouting and cursing, they run backwards, still holding their phones and filming as they sprint away.

What are you filming? the woman asks one of the protestors as they take cover next to her. *Decay*, they say, not looking up.

One of the protestors faces her. A young man, early twenties, with a crew cut. His fresh white T-shirt, sleeves rolled up, is splattered with coin-size droplets of blood. Head cocked, he squints his eyes. She watches him study her face.

Hey, he asks, *do I know you from somewhere?*

Yes, punk, she thinks to herself. My mom was all over the news ten years ago. If you want, I could puke vulture feathers all over your shoes.

No, she says slowly and carefully, *I don't think we've met.*

She observes the baseball bat in his hands, currently swinging loose and innocent near his waist. She imagines him beating her into submission then binding her wrists and tying her up somewhere public. Dousing her with cow's blood and bird feathers and calling her a psycho bird murderer like her mother. While a crowd of onlookers point and laugh like wild animals.

Must be confusing you with someone else.

Happens all the time.

He grins. Sweating from her face, she smiles back. A bead of sweat drips into her eye socket, stinging her eyeball, temporarily blurring the scene in front of her.

SCREW THAT LIBERAL HAIR, a sign propped against a skyscraper reads. The protestors now throwing trash at the bloody vulture. *Fly, birdy, fly*, they heckle the bird.

Standing there, watching them berate the vulture, she can feel something harden on her legs. Looking down, she sees the dark reflective glass of the skyscraper. Covering each of her shinbones in two long, black, glassy strips.

Clenching her fists into balls, she flees the scene. Heading back toward her apartment. Climbing the winding stairs, her shins roar with each step as the glass abrades the skin on her legs. When she arrives at the door, she pauses, looking down at her shins. There the glossy stripes remain. She closes her eyes, breathes through her nose, and begins counting down from four. Trying to erase the image of the man's disgusted face.

Four . . . three . . . two . . . one . . . eventually her leg becomes skin again. No more glass. She enters the apartment to find the man moored to the couch, his ear pressed against the air-conditioning box. His fingertips shine with grease. An empty plate at his feet.

As she stands in the entryway, she feels her boundaries flickering. One glass stripe reappears on her shin in a painful burst.

There's something black on your leg.

I know. A hard rock forms in her throat. She focuses her attention out the window: a cloud moves slowly, slowly across the lapis-blue sky.

I just bought soap, he says.

I don't know if it'll work, her voice creaks like a faucet.

Oh, he says, uninterested. *Did you figure out why they are protesting?*

I dunno.

You don't know? He grabs the arm of the couch.

Something to do with POP'S COLA, she shrugs.

He scowls, rising from the love seat.

His face affronts hers. He cinches his bathrobe; his breath smells like tar.

You hardly have a clue. He lunges forward, then pauses, hesitating before he wraps his hands around her neck. She feels the skin on her neck folding. Oxygen narrowing, as the pressure tightens. She begins to count down from ten. If I get to one and his hands are still on my neck, she thinks, I will ask him to stop.

You work for a megacorporation that stole your mother's freedom. Yet you think of yourself as a victim.

The woman pictures herself stepping back in the entryway, allowing the blue-uniforms to march inside. *I am a victim*, she says dryly, trying to breathe. As his hands squeeze the air from her throat.

That's not the point. He tightens his clasp—her cheeks grow pink.

Heat spreads like a rash up her stomach to her breasts and face. The light washes in her eyes, as she remembers the blue-uniforms with their wire, how Momma had cried out while they wrapped her feet together. Today, the light is too bright, fluorescent, thick.

The man continues, *When our institutions fail us, individually we assume the burden of changing—*

She spits before she can really think.

Her saliva shoots out her mouth in a ball, lifting off her tongue and landing onto the man's cheek. His grasp relaxes as his lips struggle to form words. Her spittle stuck to his right cheek, a glob with a white crest and foamy bubbles.

He touches her spit with his index finger, then holds his glistening finger up to his face. A ribbon of saliva falls from his finger onto the floor.

His expression assembles itself on his face. Arched brows, blue eyes churning. He sucks one breath in. Avoiding her eyes, he wipes the spit on his jeans with the flat of his hand.

Wordlessly, he staggers out the apartment.

THE WOMAN GETS HOME FROM THE COLA HOTEL. IN THEIR STUDIO APARTMENT, THE MAN IS DRESSED AS ELVIS.

An Elvis wig that grows wild at the crown. A yellow lei made of plastic blossoms. The man gazes at himself in the long mirror. She emerges from behind his reflection. His eyes flick past her balled-up COLA uniform in her hand.

Moving backward, he says, *You and I live in a different world.*

Makes her want to shout. She stays put. The building-breaking feeling. Inside a glossed stare. Focusing on the man's pearly white buttons. The tiny thickets of hair on her eyebrows: a little patch growing disordered. Sweat cooling on her collarbones. Might burst.

The man prances back, frightened by something he sees, almost knocks into her. The woman hangs briefly in the air, frozen.

A pigeon passing in a dead, black streak beyond the window. She closes her eyes and sees the bird passing behind the screen of her lids.

She roams over to the couch and clicks on the TV. She's trying to relax into a state of unseeing. A news anchor, headlines running at the bottom of the screen. The man strides over to shut the window.

Did you leave this open? he says.

I'm not sure, she says, watching a female on-screen sip a POP'S COLA.

He says, *When you leave the window open, you waste good energy. Do you ever think about the consequences of your actions?* He slams the window hard, shaking the little black table.

Come here, he orders.

She rises, hands shaking. *Where?*

Over here. He points at the window, his voice quiet and controlled. Slowly she creeps toward him as his eyes glitter. Up close, she notices the stubs of his beard hair growing on his cheeks and chin. His breath is minty and fresh as he coils his right hand across her wrist. The man's fingers squeeze her wrist bones, making her flesh bulge around his grip.

She pictures herself riding the train back to Pinecoast. Toward the house where she grew up alone. An entirely silent house. Aside from its gurgling pipes and whistling floorboards. Her breath shakes, not from the man's rough touch, but from the memory of silence.

The yellow home the yellow home t h e y e l l o w h o m e . . .

His grip narrows on her wrist. Fragments of pain run up her arm. She closes her eyes and braces herself. All the muscles in her face tense. Would he hit her cheeks first? Would he break her cheekbones into ribbons? Keeping her eyes shut, she can smell the Elvis enclave: the dried sweat, desert air, and whiskey beneath his minty breath.

Shutting her eyes so hard, orange-and-green shapes begin to explode behind her lids like fireworks. When she opens her eyes, they catch on the yellow flowers on the counter. The petals wilted, saggy, and brown.

The woman thinks of her aunt. The woman remembers sitting across from her at the diner as her aunt removed three crumpled yellow roses from her purse. Handing them to her, a gift. Her aunt regarding her as the woman sniffed the roses, her aunt's eyes dark and motionless like glass. Watching her aunt drive away, her red car receding on the road, the woman had felt nothing. No pain, no anguish. Not even a tight chest or a trembling lip—totally numb.

To her surprise, the man's fingers relax on her wrist. The slivers of pain abate as his hand loosens, then drops away. The man steps backward, quickly, as the woman twists her sore wrist in circles.

I'm leaving, he says quietly.

Turning away, he reaches to grab his binder of Elvis lyrics. Bending down, he sees a single white feather on the floor beneath the couch. He picks the feather up. Eyes lit, he spindles the shaft of the feather in his fingers.

A wry smile creeps over his face like a shadow.

The woman squeezes her fingers into her palms, pushing her pointy nails into her doughy flesh. Earlier that day, she'd gotten herself so worked up about the man, she'd broken out in a film of wren feathers, some of which had molted as she strode around the apartment. She thought she'd removed the evidence but forgot to check under the couch.

She doesn't respond to the man. His smile trembles, as if pained, then he turns. Still holding the feather, he hurls the front door shut. The apartment shakes. His boots thud quietly down the shared hall of the complex.

Inhale. She counts to four and absorbs the room around her. The man's white jumpsuit, rumpled, strewn on the arm of the couch. Petals from his Hawaiian lei lay on the floor alongside crumpled pages of song lyrics. His soda cans and burrito wrappers stuffed under the coffee table.

Then, on the floor near the table, she notices something. Her potted plant overturned on the floor, dirt clotted on the surrounding wood. In its place, the Elvis statuette stands in the center of the table. Her precious plant had been replaced by the man's statue of Elvis.

The feelings that register in the woman are slow to rise to the surface. Hearing only what silence allows you to observe. The clock on the wall ticks, the water rushes through the pipes, her cell phone dings on the table. On the street, a cow groans.

She hobbles over to her bed, off-balance. She spreads herself across the mattress, opening her arms across the cool duvet.

At the end of this movie, she thinks, there is a yellow house near the sea. There has to be. She closes her eyes and pictures it.

AT THE END OF HER SHIFT AT THE COLA HOTEL, MR. BOSS CALLS THE WOMAN INTO HIS OFFICE.

Sit. She obeys.

I've received a complaint about some ash residue on COLA sculpture number twenty-one. Did you scrub that sculpture?

Mr. Boss drums his finger on his desk.

I'm not sure which one that is. The woman pulls her uniform away from her neck and shoulders, grating her teeth.

The glass sculpture? Mr. Boss says.

They're all glass.

This one is particularly glassy. It's unmistakable—

A knock bellows from the door behind her. Mr. Boss checks his wristwatch and frowns. *Excuse me.*

Advancing toward the knock, he jerks the door open a crack, whispering to his long-legged secretary who peeks through the slit. The woman hears the secretary hush the word: *Elvis.*

While they whisper, the woman studies the purple Siamese fighting fish in the aquarium facing the wall. Their purple fins flash in clear water.

Is someone waiting for you? she says when he returns to his desk.

Don't worry about my schedule. If you leave my COLA bottles dirty in the future, you won't have a job. I've put a note in your file. Get out.

She blinks, stunned. She sees a magenta flash above the tank. Then a berry-colored fish, the length of a toothpick, flies out the tank and onto the office carpet. Every few seconds, the Siamese fighting fish hops a few inches off the gray, flat surface.

She freezes, inhales deeply, and covers her mouth as the fish flops on the floor. Mr. Boss runs over to the fish and, holding the woman's gaze, he stomps it dead.

Looking at her with snarled lips, he says, *Bye.*

Standing, she blushes. She holds the anger and confusion between her shoulder blades, striding out of his office. As the image of the wriggling magenta fish rewinds and replays in her mind: its limp fins splayed on the dirty office carpet.

In the waiting room, she's surprised to see the man, wearing his bejeweled jumpsuit, perched in a chair. Fidgeting with a plastic bag containing his Elvis wig.

What are you doing here? she says.

I can't talk now, he rises. *Wait for me out front.*

THE WOMAN EXITS THE POP'S COLA HOTEL AND WAITS ON THE SIDEWALK NEAR THE MAN'S CAR.

Perched on the hot curb, she surveys the landscape. In front of the stucco walls of the COLA Hotel, a cow eats a dead vulture, its tongue lapping up feathers. For a second, the cow glances up at her, sneers. A strand of white intestine dangles from its mouth like a deflated inner tube. Blood smeared across its white lips.

Layers of heat shimmer up from the pavement. Each breath feels like war waged against the hot, wet air. Even her scalp and ears are sweaty and slick. Her white uniform, drenched, sticks to her body like a wet towel.

The man appears outside the white stucco walls and raises his arm in greeting. *Hey*, he calls out, *I'll unlock the car.*

The black car wobbles as the woman gets inside. Within minutes, the man joins her.

What were you meeting Mr. Boss about? she says as he slides into the driver's seat.

Nothing that concerns you.

The car engine rumbles as they glide away from the hotel. The air-conditioning at first blows hot air as the engine warms up. Eventually, the artificial breeze turns cold. The woman suspends her head in front of the vent and lets the cold draft hit her in the face. When they stop at a streetlight, the man rolls down the window to toss out a soda can. A triangle of ash snakes inside the car, and the man sucks it inside his mouth. He rolls the window up after the soda can hits the pavement with a light thud.

Have you ever considered going to therapy? he asks as the car pauses at a red light.

Why? A brown cow clumsily advances toward the car. As the sedan waits at the light, the cow knocks its gaunt head against her passenger window. Thump, thump, thump. The light switches to green. As they rush ahead, the cow's bleating fades into the backdrop.

Lately you've become moody and irate, the man says. *You don't have any fulfillment outside of me.*

His palms wrapped across the steering wheel, skin tight across his knuckles. She rolls down her window, which the heat snakes through, scalding her face.

That's not true.

You're so disconnected, you have no idea how dangerous you are.

Don't you think the same message could apply to you? she says, in her mind seeing the fish flop on the office carpet, gasping for breath.

We're here, the man says.

He opens the car door. Heat penetrates the black interior like a punch in the face. *Come on*, he says, *I want to show you something.*

Where are we going? she says, sweating as they struggle down a sand path.

You'll see, the man says, grabbing her hand as they walk up a hill of sand. Struggling as her feet sink and sand fills her sneakers. Finally, they reach the top of the slope. There, the woman sees an abandoned concrete pool filled with garbage.

They slide down the hill toward the concrete reservoir. When they reach the base, they kick away a bag of trash to make room to sit on the ledge. *It smells*, the woman says, inhaling sour rot. The man throws a pebble into the pool, which thuds lightly against a garbage bag. Heaps of trash spot the dry reservoir. Plastic bags, tinfoil, cans, wrappers, Styrofoam, a disemboweled black sneaker. A slight wind blows the scent of a rotting animal corpse from the deep end of the pool. The woman plugs her nose.

This place has been empty for years, the man says, *I thought you needed to see it yourself.*

Why?

So you can see supporting a company that pollutes is wrong. This means quitting your job.

Why are you bringing this up now? She lifts the edge of her uniform to dab the sweat from her face.

I'm just trying to help you understand it's not about you. There are people less fortunate than you who will suffer, the man says.

I've suffered too. She crosses her arms.

His lips set in a line; he digs one heel of his alligator boot into the sand. Then his phone buzzes in his pocket and he whispers, *Hello.*

The absence of his warm body beside her. He strides to the far edge of the reservoir, almost out of earshot. The sun hides behind a cloud. From a distance, she hears traces of the man's whispering and the rustling of rats.

Across the reservoir, he meets her eyes with no expression. Goose bumps sprout on her skin, little white soldiers. After he hangs up the phone, they stalk back to the car in silence. Listening to his boots slide in the sand, crunching over bird bones and small rocks. His head turned down, focusing on the ground below his boots.

There should be a word for this particular type of silence. Zombie silence. The silence where you have no idea—at all—what the other person is thinking. She looks up into the sky—blue, wide, birdless—listening to the eerie scrunch of their shoes against sand.

AFTER HER SHIFT, THE MAN MEETS THE WOMAN NEAR THE COLA HOTEL. ON THE WAY TO DINNER, HE ASKS TO STOP INSIDE A CANDY STORE.

Can we head home? the woman says, *I'd like to change my shoes before dinner. My feet hurt.*

It'll just take a minute. He grins so wide it splits his face.

Turning, he smooths his wig and starts to enter the store.

The man approaches a calf stretched across the store entrance. The calf whines as the man kicks its leg with his boot. She follows him, careful to avoid stepping on the whimpering animal.

Don't do that, she says.

He was blocking the path.

Walking down the aisle, she admires candy wedding rings, the color of smudged pink, piled in a glass case. The man retrieves one candy ring from the pile and swivels toward her.

He sinks down on one knee and thrusts the candy wedding ring in the air. The woman fidgets with her skirt pockets. Unsure of what is happening, she stops breathing, though her cheeks prepare to flush.

A wave of nervous heat floods her feet. She bites her lip and wiggles her fingers at her sides as she hesitates. Then, slowly, she outstretches her hand, heart pulsing in her throat. She lifts her ring finger so he can slide the candy up it.

Then the man leaps to his feet, sending his Elvis wig lopsided. *Just kidding*, he deposits the candy ring back inside the case. *I always wanted to do that with a fake ring.* She breathes out. Her posture softens as the air in her body deflates. The man saunters a few feet ahead of her and doesn't look back.

Three blue-uniforms materialize in the candy store window. Dark, expressionless eyes; white trapezoid-shaped badges. One blue-uniform shades his eyes with his palm as he inspects the store. Pointing at the woman, *There she is.* The other blue-uniforms begin to file inside.

The woman turns to the man, *What is happening?*

The man's face is entirely unreadable. *I guess they must think you're a terrorist.* His eyes glint on the blue-uniforms making a beeline toward her.

Her breath shortens in her lungs. Listening to their heavy boots smack the floor as they lunge toward her.

Could it be true. It had to be. But it wasn't yet.

When the first blue-uniform apprehends the woman, he pushes her against a wall. He reaches for his wire. She tries to wiggle free as he restrains her flailing arms.

I'm not a gull terrorist, she says as he grabs her left wrist and twists until she yelps. The blue-uniform shoves her against the wall, knocking her head back against the wood. Hard. For a second, the sound gets sucked from her ears; her blood pressure drops; her knees sink. A hissing sound wraps itself around her mind. In the air, she wobbles.

Get on the floor. Somewhere inside of her, she gives in. As she stands there, not responding, the blue-uniform slaps her. Hard. Her legs begin to collapse.

As she slumps to the ground, she has the familiar, sinking feeling she is on-screen. When her right cheek hits the cold ground, it is only the climax of an awesome film.

One blue-uniform kicks her wiggling trunk. *Help*, she cries out. A crowd surrounds them, a half circle of observers, but no one responds.

Wearing tall black boots, the blue-uniform strikes the woman's face, drawing blood from her lip. Then steps back. Her ears ring like a siren, above the hissing and the pain. (The past, it will recycle and repeat itself. Do not try to resist it. Your biology makes it so.)

You have been accused of the murder of a wren at the High Plains sand park on the afternoon of June . . .

One blue-uniform wraps copper wire around her ankles.

While the man melds into the crowd gathering around her, she sees only his calves dotted with fake, gold slippers. He stares, watching, not protesting.

More people gather around her. As the blue-uniforms bind her feet, she hears the crinkle of a plastic candy being unwrapped. As the wire starts to cut into her skin, she hears the beep of someone's cell phone recording her. The ground rumbles as the audience swells. In the crowd, somebody chews popcorn. Someone jokingly claps. Someone gasps. The woman shuts her eyes, tasting the metal of her blood as it trickles out the corner of her mouth.

The crowd grows restless as the violence stalls.

One by one, the people disperse.

THE BLUE-UNIFORMS DRAG HER OUT OF THE CANDY STORE.

Holding the woman by the pits, the blue-uniforms pull her down the sidewalk, wire wrapped tight around her feet. The hard copper digs into her flesh. Her bound feet scrape against the concrete, bumping over rocks and soda cans and plastic bags. Their fingers dig into her shoulders as they yank her along.

Spotting the man exiting the store. Slow, unhurried; his gaze clear. A pit in the woman's stomach hardens. Their stares meet.

I suppose, she thinks, I always expected bad things to happen.

His gaze blank, the man doesn't wave or nod. For a second, she tries to squirm free. The man stops walking. And so the space between them widens. She moves forward, tugged.

A bitterness rises up in her throat, acidic, green. She remembers Momma's ash-stained fingers choking the chain-link fence. But now remembering, the woman wants to punch Momma's face. Just like she wants to wrap her hands around the man's throat. Crushing his larynx. Until his skin goes blue and he can no longer sing. They both betrayed her, abandoned her, left her to chatter mindlessly with plants. All alone.

The blue-uniforms yank her across the street. A bus brakes at a traffic light and blots the man out.

A rage, blissful as it rises, unencumbered, up her esophagus and throat, emerging as a pure scream through her lips. Her cry. Shakes surviving birds from a nearby tree. Their shapes make black streaks as they rise and shiver off. Her body shakes. Blaring and fighting. She remembers her mother braiding her hair while they watched the morning news. The scream leaves her mouth as hot air, scalding her throat. The muscles in her neck on fire, straining.

While the woman screams, people's heads swivel and stare; from their perspective, she fights back. Uselessly. Against a machinery that will always crush her. To them, she is repulsive, uncontained, spit flying from her mouth, hair wild.

Cursing, she wrestles an arm free and slaps one blue-uniform's shoulder; no one flinches.

Will the van be pitch black like Momma said? Will I put my feet in somebody's eyes and not notice? Will I lose my humanity? Will it be stripped from me?

Above her head, the departing birds, she can hear their wings flapping as they rise. Their dark wings fill the sky.

In the air, their black figures freeze. The birds dive down toward the woman. Instinctively, she ducks her head and tries to curl into herself. Beside her, the blue-uniforms tense.

But she doesn't feel the bird claws on her arms, doesn't feel their beaks, sharp as rusty scissors, cutting her face. Doesn't sense wet blood dripping down her ears or feel their hook-beaks slicing up her neck.

Out of the corner of her eye, she sees one crow plunge its beak into the blue-uniform's neck; a little spray of blood dribbles out. The blue-uniform howls. He places his hand on his neck to try and staunch the bleeding. Both blue-uniforms let go of her arms as they defend themselves against the bloodthirsty crows.

Unharmed, the woman steps back.

The blue-uniform tries to swat and distract the shrieking hoard of black feathers, talons, and beaks. As the crows squawk and bite and poke. Blood drips onto the sidewalk. The blue-uniforms try to shield their soft necks and heads, but there are too many birds, and their black beaks, gleaming in the sunlight, are too quick.

One crow grabs the blue-uniform's earlobe with its beak, rips out the flesh, and swallows the soft part of his ear. The blue-uniform shrieks, swatting at the bird and catching the blood with his palms. Plummeting to the sidewalk, the blue-uniforms cover their ears with their bloodied hands, crying out. The birds' black feathers refract the sunlight as they work their beaks into soft, exposed flesh. Nipping, pulling, biting. The blood of the blue-uniforms darkens the pavement.

More black birds swarm the air. As they cloud the sky, their shadows dance on the sidewalk. The atmosphere thickens with the shrieks of feeding birds. The blue-uniforms moan and writhe like baby snakes, kicking their legs against the sidewalk as they beg for mercy.

The woman smiles. The birds, they aren't lying down, but fighting back. They are the rats of the air.

Closing her eyes, she pictures the sea lions lounging, serenely, on the zoo rock. She can hear them barking like dogs. She feels the hot dog wrapper in her hand, the smooth unraveling of waves, her aunt's soft palm inside her own, which, out of nowhere, suddenly let go.